Shanti Fights for Her Rights

Shanti Fights for Her Rights

Marcia E. Barss

Shanti Fights for Her Rights
Copyright© 2023 Marcia E. Barss

All rights reserved under international copyright conventions. No part of this publication may be reproduced, stored in or introduced into a retrieval system, or transmitted in any form, or by any means, without the prior written permission of the author.

First published in 2023 by

Halifax, NS, Canada
www.ocpublishing.ca

Cover and interior book design by David W. Edelstein
Cover illustration by Sneha Roy

ISBN 978-1-989833-32-2 (Paperback edition)
ISBN 978-1-989833-36-0 (eBook edition)

Reviews
Shanti Fights for Her Rights

"Shanti features a feisty yet sympathetic and relatable main character, a compelling plot, and lots of authentic detail about the challenging lives of girls and women in rural India. This timely and well-written story will have readers cheering Shanti and her friends on, as they fight for their rights to an education and an end to child marriage. Just like me, both children and adults will love and learn from this heartfelt book!"

Vivien Gorham,
author of *Touch of Gold* and *Spirit of Summerwood*

"A beautifully detailed, suspenseful story about a young girl fighting to free herself from an impossible situation. Shanti's courage in standing up for her rights against the culture of her community and her family's wishes helps other girls do the same and shows how one voice can make a difference."

Jacqueline Halsey, author of *Piper*

*To girls all over the world
who fight for their right to education,
and to those who support them
in achieving their dreams.*

Preface

Child marriage is a concern in many countries. A UNICEF report in 2021 stated that one in five girls is married before the age of eighteen, the legal age for marriage. Early marriage often results in early pregnancy, which puts a girl's health at risk. Complications from pregnancy and childbirth are the second leading cause of death for girls under fifteen years of age.

In India, thousands of girls marry before they are eighteen. Child marriage persists in India for several reasons, including tradition, poverty, gender discrimination, and disregard for the law.

In Telangana, India, where this story is set, Dr. Mamatha Achanta started Tharuni, an organization to support girls and promote their education. Tharuni worked with UNICEF to establish balika sanghas (girls' groups), and there are now hundreds of sanghas with thousands of girls as members. Girls in these groups gain self-confidence and are supported in continuing their education, and they work together to stop child marriages. Like Shanti, they feel empowered to stand up for their rights.

Chapter One

I poured water from the bucket into my brass pot and handed the bucket to my friend Danya. Two other girls were chatting at the well, waiting for a turn to fill their pots.

"I have to hurry home," I said, placing the pot on my head. "The midwife thinks my mother will deliver the baby very soon."

"I'll walk with you," Danya said. "I'm glad the baby waited until we were on holidays."

I laughed. "My mother and grandmother are glad too, so I can help with everything for a few weeks. I'm excited about the baby, but I'd rather be away at school where we don't have to carry water and wash clothes in the river and cook meals over a smokey fire."

"It'll be years before life in our village is more like life in town," Danya said as we walked on the dirt path between rows of houses, some with brick walls and tin roofs, others with mud walls and roofs of thatched palm leaves.

"I heard one of the girls at school saying that her village finally got mobile service," I said. "Let's hope we'll get a cellphone tower near our village soon. It'd be fun to phone our friends when we're home on holidays."

We were near my home when we heard a long wail. "That came from your house," Danya said.

I put both hands on my pot to keep it balanced on my head as I hurried home. Chickens scattered out of my way when I stepped onto our veranda. I set the pot down and paused at our doorway, which was covered with a sari when my mother started in labour. I heard a baby's cry.

"Mother? May I come in?"

"Yes, come," the midwife answered.

I held the sari back and entered the shadowy room. The smell of blood was the first thing I noticed. "Is the baby okay? Are you?"

"Oh, Shanti, another girl. I'm so unlucky," my mother wailed.

"Shh," said the midwife as she gently wrapped the squirming baby in a towel. She placed her in my arms and turned back to attend to my mother. My grandmother was cleaning up the mess from the birthing.

Tears filled my eyes as I looked at the baby's face. "She's beautiful. I'm happy to have a little sister."

"No, no, your father will be so angry I didn't give him a son," my mother moaned.

My grandmother shook her head and muttered, "He'll soon find a husband for Shanti."

I was stunned. Father couldn't do that to me. "But I'm only fourteen. I'm doing well in school, and it's against the law for girls to get married before they're eighteen."

My grandmother grunted. "That doesn't matter in our village. Your sister was married at your age. Balamani didn't need school to learn how to cook and look after her husband."

I pressed my lips together so I wouldn't say something disrespectful. I looked at my new sister. She opened her dark eyes wide and gazed at me. Love filled my heart and I smiled at her. "Don't listen to them, little one," I whispered. "We'll show them girls can do anything. We must have big dreams. I promise I'll do my best at school and teach you everything I can."

"Shanti, bring the baby to your mother to feed," the midwife said. She settled my sister against my mother's breast. I was amazed at how such a tiny baby knew what to do to get milk.

My mother smiled as she gently ran her

fingers over the baby's cheek. "She looks like you did, Shanti." I hoped she wouldn't say anything more about wanting a boy.

"Finish cleaning up here, Shanti," my grandmother ordered. "I'll go tend to the fire and look after cooking our supper."

The midwife asked for a basin of warm water to bathe the baby. I brought it to her and watched while she gently cleaned my sister. She wrapped her in a soft cloth and tucked her beside my mother. As we tidied the room the midwife said, "Shanti, why do you want to stay in school?"

"I want to be a teacher, or maybe a nurse."

My grandmother heard me and muttered, "Humph! Forget your dreams. You'll soon be married like your sister and keep house for your in-laws."

I bit my lip to keep from arguing with her. I would just have to prove her wrong.

A few hours later I was sweeping the front yard when I saw my father returning from working in the rice field. He'd know the baby had arrived, as news travels quickly in our village. From his slow walk, I was sure he knew the baby was a girl. He would have been striding down the path, shouting out to all the neighbours if he now had a son.

"*Namaste*, Father," I greeted him, smiling, though my belly was tight with worry over what he'd say. "Mother and the new baby are doing well. Come see them."

"Hmm. So she had another girl," he said, going into our house. My mother and the baby were sleeping. My father looked at them and let out a long sigh. Then he walked through the back doorway, stopping by his mother, who was squatting by the fire stirring the vegetable stew. My grandmother said something about marriage. Father murmured a reply as he washed his hands, but I couldn't hear what he said.

My grandmother called to me, "Shanti, come and serve your father supper." I took a tin plate off the shelf where we kept our few dishes. She spooned rice onto it, then scooped some spicy vegetable stew on top. I placed it in front of my father, who was sitting on a mat on the floor opposite the bed where my mother still slept.

When he finished, I brought him tea. He took a sip. "Another girl to feed. Another dowry," he muttered. "I'll have to find a husband for you, Shanti."

I slapped my hand over my mouth to hold back my scream.

"You don't need any more education. You'll stay home and look after the baby. Then your mother can get back to working in the fields."

"Oh, Father, I *must* go to school," I pleaded, clenching my fists. My mother had wakened and was watching us. I looked from my mother to my father and back to Mother, afraid that if I let one word out, I'd explode in a mess of emotions.

My mother's eyes met mine. I couldn't give up school and stay home as my father demanded. And I refused to get married. I'm sure she hoped I wouldn't say anything more. She must have wished for some kind words from my father about the baby. Couldn't he say something nice to her? Surely he'd accept the baby when he saw how sweet she was.

My father sighed, shook his head slowly, and walked across the small room to my mother. She had propped herself up on one elbow on the bed, and the baby still slept beside her.

I held my breath, waiting to hear what he'd say. He knelt beside the bed and put a hand on Mother's shoulder. "Are you all right?"

My mother tipped her head to each side, showing she was okay. Then my father looked at the sleeping baby. "And the baby?"

Mother murmured, "She's fine. But I wanted to

give you a son. I'm so sorry." She bowed her head. My father grunted and turned to me.

"Get me more tea, Shanti. Ask your grandmother what chores you should do." I hadn't eaten yet, but I didn't dare remind him. I got the tea for him, and he took it outside.

My grandmother held out a plate with rice and stew. "Shanti, take this to your mother. Then bring plates for us and we will eat too." I helped Mother sit up in bed and gave her the meal. My grandmother and I sat on the mat, and I kept my eyes on my food. I didn't speak, hoping Grandmother wouldn't lecture me about obeying my father. But of course she did.

"Shanti, you must do as your father says. He is a good son to me. He has looked after our family ever since my husband died many years ago. If you get too much education, it will be difficult to find a husband for you."

I wanted to put my hands over my ears to keep from hearing my grandmother's foolish words. The baby started crying, interrupting her. I took my mother's plate away so she could feed my sister. Very politely I asked my grandmother, "Would you like your tea now?" She nodded and I got the tea for her.

I took our plates to the backyard and washed them and the cooking pots. I picked up the brass pot and asked my grandmother, "May I go now for more water?"

She grunted and waved me out the door. My father was talking with the man who lived in the house beside ours. I felt them watching me as I walked down the path to the well. Maybe Father was already asking him if he knew of a suitable husband for me.

The sun was peeking between pink and orange clouds. The rice fields were a bright green in the evening light. A flock of parrots squawked loudly in the palmyra trees at the edge of the fields. It was so beautiful, it made me feel more hopeful after my grandmother's scolding and the talk of marriage.

Chapter Two

When I arrived at the well that evening, Danya and Trupti were there ahead of me, waiting to fill their pots. Trupti was going to be married soon even though she's only fifteen.

"How is your mother?" Danya asked me. "Is the baby okay?"

Before I could answer, Trupti said, "My mother said your grandmother is angry it's not a boy. My sister just had a boy, and they had a great celebration at his naming ceremony."

I wanted to throw water in her face, but I ignored her. I said to Danya, "She's perfect. Come and see her tomorrow." I felt like saying my father was very happy, but Trupti would know I was lying.

Trupti said, "When my neighbour had a third girl, her mother-in-law said it was bad luck to feed her. The baby died three days later."

I glared at Trupti. "Well, this baby is *good* luck,

and she'll be smart and go to school like Danya and me instead of getting married too soon like you."

"You'll probably never get married, and you'll be thrown out of your house and have nowhere to sleep!" Trupti put her water pot on her head and left.

Danya rolled her eyes at me. "Don't listen to her, Shanti. I think she's scared about her wedding and having to go live with her in-laws. But she won't admit it. We're lucky we go to a good school where they tell us we can be anything we want."

My words slipped out before I could stop them. "Oh, Danya, my father is looking for a husband for me. He said I don't need any more education."

Danya grabbed my arm. "No, Shanti! You must stay in school. You're too smart to give it up. Remember, our teacher said, 'Education is the door to our dreams, and it is our right.' We'll fight for our rights!" She emphasized her words with a karate kick, shouting, "Hah!"

Several children playing nearby stared at Danya. They'd probably never seen anyone do karate. "Come on, Shanti, let's show these kids some of the karate moves we learned at school."

I had to smile. "Not now, Danya. I have to go home. Thanks for reminding me to be strong." We put our water pots on our heads and walked to our houses.

My father was still sitting on our veranda. I was glad the well was out of his sight, as he would have said something about Danya's karate being improper. He doesn't know I'm almost as good as she is.

"You shouldn't be out alone when it's getting dark. It's not safe for young girls," he said. I wanted to show him I could defend myself with karate, but he wouldn't approve.

I took the water pot to the backyard. My grandmother was waiting for me. "What took you so long, Shanti? Come with me now. Bring that pot to dump in the field." She pointed to an old pot that my mother was using for a latrine until she was strong enough to go to the field where the village women and girls went when it was dark. No one in our village had a latrine in their yard. I followed my grandmother on the path. As she walked, she hit the ground with a stick to scare off any scorpions or snakes.

When we returned, I unrolled sleeping mats for my grandmother and myself on one side of the room. We hung a sari across the other side to give my parents a little privacy.

My mother was feeding the baby. "Shanti, bring me a clean cloth to put under the baby, and take this wet one. Rinse it out and hang it to dry."

I did as she asked, taking the wet cloth outside.

It was peaceful in our little fenced yard. Our three hens were making gentle clucking sounds in the small coop, and my goat slept in a corner near the cooking fireplace.

The sky was full of stars. One bright one twinkled, and I imagined it was telling me to be hopeful. I winked back at it, determined to dream up a plan.

My grandmother was shaking me awake. "Come, Shanti, we must go to the field before it gets light," she whispered. The cool air outside made me shiver. I could see many others squatting in the field ahead of us. I wished we had an indoor latrine like we did at school.

As we walked back to our house, my grandmother said, "Today I must work in the rice field. We need the money. I didn't get paid yesterday because I was with your mother all day. Today you'll be home with her. Take the laundry to the river and then prepare our meal. Remember to make more yogurt after you've milked the goat."

"Yes, Grandmother." It would be a day of work for me. Maybe Danya would come to the river with me and we'd have a little time for talk and fun. I smiled thinking about holding my baby sister.

My father was sitting on a mat, mumbling his prayers. I quietly went past him to the cooking area. I blew on the coals of the cooking fire and pushed in a few twigs. When there were flames, I added some dung patties and carefully placed a pot of water on the grate for tea. Then I milked our goat and set the pot of milk next to the fire.

My grandmother had heated up leftover rice. "Bring the plates," she said.

I got the plates and took my father his breakfast, saying only "Good morning" to him. When he finished, he left to work in the fields. I warmed the milk to make yogurt before eating my rice. When my grandmother left, I was happy to be alone with my mother and the baby. Mother smiled at me as I gently held my sister's tiny hand.

"Mother, please talk with Father about my school. I love my lessons and I want to learn all I can."

"Shanti, I loved going to school, too," my mother said. "But there was no high school in my village, and my father wouldn't let me walk to the school in another village. Getting married ended my education." She sighed. "I hoped Balamani would go to high school in town, but your father found a husband for her when she was fourteen."

My mother's eyes glistened with tears. "You are so smart, Shanti. I want to see you get a good education. But a woman must not go against her husband's wishes, and a girl should not argue with her father." Tears slid down her cheeks and dropped on the baby's head. She gently wiped them away.

I felt like crying too. "Oh, Mother, my teacher told us it might be hard to convince our families that education is more important than getting married early. But there must be something I can say to Father."

Through the open doorway I saw a woman coming to our house. It was Deepama, the health care worker for our village. She greeted us with her palms together. "Namaste." We returned the greeting and asked her to come in. She slid her sandals off at the door and entered.

"The midwife told me your baby arrived quickly, and she said you're doing well. She's attending a birth in another village and asked me to visit you today." Deepama smiled as she gently touched the baby's cheek. "She is lovely. Is she eating well?"

She talked with my mother and checked her and the baby. "I'd like to weigh the baby now, so we can make sure she's gaining weight when I visit again in a week. Shanti, can you help me?" She laid the baby on the scales I held for her. "Three kilos. Good." She put the baby in my mother's arms.

Deepama looked around the room and said, "Shanti must be a big help to you. Everything looks so clean. I wish others in the villages would do as well. I see so many children who are sick, and I know better sanitation would prevent much of the illness." She shook her head and sighed. "Yesterday I was in Balamani's village, and I went to see her to check on her pregnancy. She told me she miscarried two days ago."

"Oh no," my mother said. "Is she all right?"

"She is weak and feeling tired," Deepama said. "Sixteen is too young to be pregnant. I hope she won't get pregnant again for a few years." She looked from Mother to me. "Balamani is expected to look after the housework because her mother-in-law works in the fields. Could Shanti go stay with her for a little while and help with her chores?"

I was surprised by her question. "Mother needs me here. Maybe I could go in a few days if my father agrees." I looked at my mother. She said she could manage and that she would talk with my father about allowing me to go. I knew she was worried about Balamani.

"Shanti?" I turned to see Danya in our doorway. "Can I see your baby sister?"

"Come in," I said. "She's just waking up." As Danya admired the baby, I got an idea. I told Danya about Balamani. "If I go to her village for a few days, would you get water for my mother and help her prepare meals?"

Danya agreed, and Mother looked relieved. Deepama said I could go with her to Balamani's village next week. She left to visit others.

"Have you chosen a name for your baby?" Danya asked my mother.

"Her father will talk with the priest. Then it will be kept secret until her naming ceremony." The baby started crying and my mother said, "After I feed her, we both need to sleep. You girls can go get water and then take that pile of dirty clothes to wash in the river."

Danya and I took our pots to the well and brought back water to fill our large pot in the yard. I made a bundle of the clothes that needed washing and carried it on my head. Danya went to her house for laundry and met me at the river. Trupti and another girl were there, pounding clothes on the flat rocks.

It was good to talk and laugh with the others as we worked. Danya always had funny stories to tell, and she kept Trupti from making any comments about babies. After spreading the clothes on the grass to dry, I returned home.

My mother woke as I came in, and she slowly got out of bed so the baby wouldn't wake up. We worked together preparing the evening meal. I crushed spices on our special stone while she cut up vegetables.

When my father returned in the late afternoon, Mother told him about Balamani. She said Deepama suggested I go help my sister. I listened, out of his sight, at the cooking fire.

"I should not have to be concerned with Balamani," he said. "Her in-laws are responsible for her." My mother started to reply, but he stopped her. "I understand your worry. If you'll be all right here without Shanti, I will allow her to go for a few days. How can I be sure she will get there safely?"

Mother told him I would go with Deepama. He called me into the room.

"Shanti, I suppose you've heard what I said. Maybe your sister will show you how to look after a home when you're married. It is important to respect her mother-in-law, and do what she says. You will go and return with Deepama."

"Yes, Father, I will do as you say." I knew this was not a good time to talk about school.

Chapter Three

During the following days, whenever I had a few minutes free of doing housework, I held my baby sister, singing and talking to her. My father didn't say anything more about either school or marriage, and I tried to be respectful. I needed to have a plan before saying anything to him.

I woke when our rooster crowed on the day I was going to visit Balamani. I went with my mother and grandmother to the field and washed in our yard.

My mother wrapped some sweets for me to take to my sister's family and gave me several parathas for my lunch. Everything was bundled up in a blanket and tied with twine. I'd tucked my exercise book inside.

Mother hugged me and said, "Be respectful and helpful all the time. Take good care of your sister, and tell me all about her."

I kissed my baby sister, who was sleeping on the bed. "I'll miss this sweet little one."

Deepama appeared in our doorway. "Are you ready, Shanti? We want to get there before it gets too hot."

I balanced my bundle on my head and went with Deepama through my village.

We walked on a narrow dirt path on top of the low dikes between fields. Women were harvesting rice. They used a sickle to cut the stalks, which they piled into bunches.

The sun was hot and I could feel sweat trickling down my back. I heard hoopoe birds calling and saw a flock of parrots fly toward a row of palmyra trees. Deepama asked me about school, and I told her my father said I wasn't to return after the holidays.

"Oh, Shanti, you must go to school. There are so few people in these villages that can read and write. And we know that educating women improves conditions in the village."

"I love school. I have to persuade my father to let me continue," I told her.

"Perhaps your sister can take you to a meeting of the *balika sangha* in her village. It's a group for teenaged girls where the girls talk about their right to education and they help each other find ways to stay in school," Deepama said.

"Are they ever successful?" I asked.

"I know of one fifteen-year-old girl who didn't

want to be married, and the girls talked with the school headmaster who contacted the UNICEF fieldworker. Together they convinced the parents to postpone the marriage until their daughter finished high school."

A UNICEF worker had visited our school to talk with us about the dangers of child marriage, and she told us there are funds available to families to keep their daughters in school. Hearing Deepama's story about this girl gave me a little more confidence. I hoped I could go to a meeting with my sister.

When we arrived at the village, some children who were playing near the well asked Deepama who she was going to visit.

"We're going to see Balamani," she said. "This is her sister."

A little girl about six years old with matted hair and wearing a dirty dress said, "I live beside her." She ran ahead of us down the lane between two rows of houses with mud walls and roofs of palm leaves. At the last house she went to the doorway and called, "Balamani! Your sister is here!"

Balamani stepped out onto the raised veranda. She looked very tired but smiled when she saw me. She put her palms together to greet Deepama.

"Thank you for bringing Shanti. Will you come in? Would you like some water?"

"Thank you, I'd like a drink," Deepama said. "But I can't stay long. I have several visits to make here."

The little girl watched as we shook off our sandals and stepped inside. The dried mud floor felt cool on my bare feet. I glanced around the room, which was similar to my home. The only bed had clothes piled on top, and sleeping mats were rolled up beneath it.

My sister scooped water out of a large pot into tin cups and gave them to us.

"How are you, Balamani?" Deepama said. "I was worried when you were so weak a few days ago. When I told your mother, she agreed Shanti could come to help you."

"I'm feeling stronger. My mother-in-law insisted I stay home, though my husband said I should work in the fields."

"You are lucky to have a thoughtful mother-in-law, especially one who will stand up to her son," said Deepama. "If she says your sister can stay, I'll be here again in a week, and I can take Shanti back to her village with me. Let Shanti do any lifting for you. Now I must get on with my visits. Namaste."

When she left, Balamani hugged me. "I'm so glad you're here. I miss you all so much. How is Mother?"

I told her all about the new baby. "They are both doing well, and our father too." I didn't mention that he was very displeased the baby was a girl.

I showed her the bundle I'd brought. "I have extra clothes for a few days. Mother sent some sweets as a gift for your in-laws." I unpacked the sweets as well as my lunch.

"I hope my mother-in-law will let you stay," said Balamani. "I feel too weak to work in the fields, and I have trouble doing the cleaning and cooking. There are clothes to be washed, but I can't carry them to the pond and wash them all." She brushed tears from her eyes.

"I could help with the washing now," I said. "Can you walk with me to the pond and sit in some shade while I do it?"

Balamani nodded. I gathered the clothes and made them into a bundle that I put on my head. We walked to the pond at the edge of the village. Several girls were there, washing their families' clothes. Two little boys splashed at one end of the pond. An older boy washed a water buffalo standing in the pond near them.

I squatted beside a flat washing stone and dipped

a shirt in the cloudy water. "Our river is much clearer than this. Will the clothes really get cleaner washed in this water?"

Balamani smiled. "Yes, just rinse them well and the sun will do the rest."

She squatted beside me and washed smaller things. We chatted with the other girls as we worked. After spreading everything out to dry on the grass, we returned to the house. Balamani sighed as she sat down on a mat to rest.

"What's my next job, sister?" I felt happy I could help.

"You could take that pot to the well and bring back water for cooking supper. Then we'll cook lentils and chop vegetables for stew."

I carried the pot in my arms and went to the well in the middle of the village. On the way I saw little girls gathering cow dung in baskets. One girl was mixing the dung with straw to make patties that she stuck to the mud walls of a house to dry.

Two girls my age were at the well, waiting their turn to drop the bucket in and fill their pots with water. They asked me lots of questions about my village and family. When I got back to Balamani's house, her mother-in-law, Bhanu, was there. She greeted me.

"I was working in the field, and I was told you came to visit your sister," she said. "Balamani said you did most of the washing and will help prepare our meal. Can you stay for a few days until she's feeling stronger?"

I nodded.

"Good. I must return to the field now. Balamani is an excellent cook. She'll guide you well."

After Bhanu left, we ate the lunch Mother had sent. We were busy in the afternoon crushing spices, peeling vegetables, and preparing supper. We had so much to talk about. Balamani told me about living in this village. I told her about school and our family.

"Mother was worried when she heard you were pregnant so soon. Were you excited or scared?" I asked Balamani. "A friend's sister had a baby when she was fifteen, and it was so tiny and weak." I didn't tell her the baby had died the next day.

"I was scared," my sister said. "Don't tell anyone, but I was relieved when I miscarried. I don't want to get pregnant again for a few years."

In the late afternoon I went to the pond to get the clothes we'd left to dry in the sun. When Bhanu and her husband and son, my sister's husband, came from working in the fields, we had supper ready. I felt shy with Balamani's husband and father-in-law, but they ignored me. Bhanu served them their meal, and when they finished eating they went outside to drink their tea and talk with other men.

"Now we girls can eat, and you can tell me about your village," said Bhanu. It was fun talking together. I helped with the cleaning up afterward and swept the floor.

Bhanu draped a sari over a thin rope to curtain off one end of the room for her husband and herself. She pointed to a rolled up mat. "Shanti, you can spread this sleeping mat beside Balamani's. We'll put up another sari to give you girls a little privacy. My son will sleep on the veranda while you're here."

After we'd prepared the room for sleeping, Bhanu told me to pour water into a small pot. "It's dark enough for us to go to the field to relieve ourselves. Bring the water, Shanti." I followed her and my sister to a field where many other village women and girls were squatting. This common latrine was like the field behind my house.

Back in their house, I wrapped the blanket I'd brought around me and stretched out on the mat. I heard squeaks and rustling noises in the roof over my head and whispered to Balamani, "What's making the noise?"

"Mice have their nests up there, and there are

bats and geckos too. Don't worry, nothing is likely to fall on you." She giggled.

I was too tired to care and fell asleep listening to the howling bark of jackals in the fields.

Chapter Four

"Shanti, time to get up. We have to get to the field before it's too light." It took me a few seconds to realize it was Balamani whispering in my ear and shaking me awake. We hurried to the same field we'd been to the night before.

When we returned to the house, Bhanu served the men breakfast. She told us the tasks to be done that day at home. They all left to work in the rice fields. As we were eating rice with yogurt, a young woman carrying a baby called to Balamani from the doorway.

"I heard your sister is here to help you, Balamani," she said. "Can you two look after my baby while I go to help with threshing the rice? You can bring him to me when he needs feeding."

Balamani looked at me, and I shrugged and tipped my head in agreement. I held out my hands to the baby, and he hid his face in his mother's shoulder. When she put him in my arms he started to cry.

"He'll be fine when I'm out of sight. He can nap in the hammock on my veranda," his mother said as she left the house. The baby cried loudly and tried to wriggle free.

"What's his name?" I asked my sister as I struggled to hold on to him.

"Tilak. He lives next door," Balamani said. "Bring him to the back so he can watch the chickens while we sweep the yard and weed the garden."

I carried Tilak through the house, singing a tune that soothed my little sister. When I showed him the chickens, he stopped crying. I set him down near them but he let out a wail, so I picked him up again.

"I won't get any work done if I have to carry him around."

"I was hoping you'd milk the buffalo," Balamani said. "Maybe that can wait until Tilak falls asleep."

"Is that one of your jobs?" I asked. "I've never milked a buffalo."

"It's not much different from milking a goat," said Balamani. She started sweeping the yard. Tilak stopped crying and made a grunting sound.

Balamani looked at him and said, "Quick, Shanti, hold him away from you. I think he's pooping."

I stood him on the ground and held him under

his arms. As we watched, his poop landed on the earth. We laughed as Tilak peed, just missing my bare foot.

"Ugh, how do we clean this up?"

"Use two dung patties to pick it up and dump it in the field where we were this morning," said Balamani. "I'll wash Tilak."

I cleaned up the mess and took it to the field, being careful not to drop any on the way. When I returned I poured some water on the earth where Tilak had peed and swept it clean.

"I'm glad you warned me in time, or I'd be washing my clothes," I said to my sister.

Tilak was content splashing in a pan of water Balamani had put him in. After a while he started whimpering. I carried him to the front and placed him in the hammock his mother had made by tying a sari to the poles holding up the roof of the veranda. As I swung the hammock and sang a lullaby, he fell asleep.

"Now you can show me how to milk your buffalo," I said to Balamani.

"Bring some fresh straw from the pile over there and place it in front of her," Balamani said. "She'll be busy eating and won't mind you milking her." The buffalo was tied to a post at the end of the veranda.

Balamani showed me where to place a pail under the buffalo's teats and told me what to do.

I gently squeezed a teat in each hand. No milk came out. But the buffalo swished its tail in my face. Balamani giggled. I didn't think it was so funny.

"Squeeze firmly, Shanti. You won't hurt her."

When I squeezed the teat harder, a stream of milk squirted into the pot. It wasn't as easy as milking a goat, and my hands got tired. Finally the pail was full, and I was very pleased with myself.

"Bring the milk to the fire and we'll heat it up to make more yogurt," said Balamani. I filled a glass for each of us to drink before pouring some into a pot that I placed over the burning coals of the fire. When the milk was warm enough, I stirred it into leftover yogurt in a pan and covered it with a cloth.

"Now the big water pots need to be filled for washing and cooking," said Balamani. She gave me a smaller pot to take to the well.

On my way to the well, I saw the little girl who'd led me to my sister's house. She was wearing the same dirty dress and her hair was still uncombed. The pot she carried on her head was as big as mine.

"What's your name?" I asked.

"Meena," she said, smiling shyly.

When we got to the well, several girls were there, waiting for their turn to use the bucket.

"Where do you go to school?" I asked a girl who looked about my age.

The girl shook her head. "I don't go to school anymore. The one in our village is only for little children," she said. "My father won't allow me to walk five miles to the town for high school. We have to work in the fields or help at home looking after the younger children."

Meena and I filled our pots and walked back together. My sister was bending over Tilak, trying to soothe him back to sleep. He was struggling to get out of the hammock.

"He's awake already? That was a short nap," I said. "Will he play for a while or shall we take him to his mother for feeding?"

Tilak let out a wail and refused to be comforted.

"I guess he knows what he wants," said Balamani. "Will you carry him, Shanti? I'll walk with you to where his mother is working."

I picked him up and placed him on my hip. As we walked down the narrow pathway between the rows of houses, Balamani called out greetings to neighbours who were sweeping their yards or pounding rice into flour. When we came to the place where people were threshing the rice, we saw Tilak's mother whacking a bundle of rice straw on the ground to knock off the grains. Tilak cried out to her, and she turned to him.

"Are you hungry, little one?" she asked, reaching for him. "Now I can rest for a bit." She put him to her breast and he sucked noisily. We squatted beside them and chatted. When Tilak was finished, his mother handed him back to me.

"I'm glad you can look after him. There's so much work to do here."

We returned to Balamani's house and ate some parathas with stewed lentils for our lunch. Tilak sat on the floor and played with pebbles that he put in a pot and dumped out. We began preparations for supper, chopping vegetables we'd picked from the garden behind the house.

"Are you happy to be married?" I asked my sister.

Balamani looked directly at me. "This is my life. I have no choice." She hesitated and added, "But you're so smart and could do so many things. I hope you don't get married for a long time."

"I don't want to get married for many years! I want to go to school and take my exams so I can be a teacher." I sighed. "But Father said he is looking for a husband for me, and he gets angry when I disagree.

Mother won't say anything to help even though I know she doesn't want me to get married now."

"If we were boys we wouldn't have these problems," said Balamani. "They can do what they want. And when they marry, their wife does everything for them."

"I have to think of a way to stop Father from trying to marry me off."

"We have a group here where the girls meet and help each other with their problems," my sister said. "You can come with me to the next meeting."

"Deepama told me about that."

"We have fun at the meetings, too," Balamani said. "Right now I need to lie down and rest. Tilak might sleep again, if you rock him in the hammock. Then you can do whatever you want for a while."

Tilak didn't protest at all when I put him in the hammock, and he was soon asleep. I sat in the shade on the veranda and opened my exercise book. My teacher had told us to write an essay over the holidays, and I started writing about my baby sister.

Meena came with an older woman she said was her grandmother. "Meena said you go to school," the woman said. "Can you write a letter for me? No one in my family can write, and I want to tell my son about his father's illness. My son left to work in

Visakhapatnam, and he hasn't been back to visit in many months."

"Yes, I can write a letter," I said. "I'll use a page from my exercise book. What do you want to say?" The woman told me what to write, and I suggested some words. When I finished I read the letter to the woman.

She smiled and said, "That's good. I'll give you five rupees. Now I'll take the letter to be posted." She gave me the money, and she and Meena left.

I was busy writing in my notebook when another woman stopped to talk with me.

"Harchini said you wrote a letter for her. Will you write one for me?"

I agreed and used another page from my notebook to write a letter for this woman. She paid me five rupees as well. Balamani came out when she heard the talking.

The woman said to her, "Your sister is very clever. She wrote a good letter for me." After the woman left, I showed my sister the money I'd been given.

"Do you think I could earn money at home writing letters for people? Maybe that would show Father that education is useful."

"You could try that, Shanti," Balamani replied.

"It's time now to finish cooking supper. The others will be coming home soon."

As I lay on my mat that night, I thought about the letter-writing idea and wondered if it might help change my father's mind about letting me return to school.

Chapter Five

The next morning when I was sweeping the floor, Meena peeked in the doorway.

"Are you going to write more letters today?"

"Maybe later. We have lots of work to do first," I said.

"I can help you with your work," Meena said. "I've already finished what my grandmother told me to do. She went to help with the threshing."

"I'm going to milk the buffalo next, and then Balamani and I are going to wash our hair. Would you like us to help you wash yours?" When I first met Meena I thought how pretty she'd look with clean hair and clothes. I wondered why no one looked after her.

Meena grinned and nodded. "I can finish the sweeping for you so you can do the milking now."

I gave her the broom and got the pail for the milking. I told Balamani the plan, and she was happy to have the little girl join us. "I feel sorry for Meena," she said. "Her mother died a few years ago, and her grandmother works most days in the fields, so no one has time for her."

I was quicker milking the buffalo this time. Meena squatted beside me, chatting about people in the village. I had just finished milking when the buffalo raised its tail and pooped, leaving a steaming pile of dung on the straw.

"Yuck!" I said, leaning away.

Meena jumped up and got her basket that she'd left in the yard. She scooped the dung into the basket with her hands. She mixed in pieces of straw to make a firm lump. She took a handful and expertly patted it into a flat cake. She slapped the dung cake on the mud wall of the house and started to make another.

"You make those patties faster than anyone I've seen," I said.

"I'm the best in the village," she declared.

I carried the pail of milk to Balamani so she could make yogurt. I brought a small pot of water to Meena. "When you've finished, you can wash your hands and then come into the backyard. You can take some milk home later."

"Are you going to wash your hair now?"

I nodded. "We'll wait for you. Be sure to wash your hands well."

Balamani and I discussed what to do with Meena's hair, whether to try to comb out the tangles first or give it a good wash. When she came to the backyard, I was ready with a comb, and she sat on the ground in front of me. As I worked through her matted hair, she chattered away and didn't complain when the comb caught in the tangles.

"You could wash your dress too," Balamani said. "Can you go get another to put on while it dries?"

Meena shook her head. "This is the only one I have." She pulled it over her head. "But it'll dry fast."

She laughed when the soapsuds from her hair ran down her back, and she scrubbed herself with them. She worked hard washing her dress and laid it in the sun. I put her hair into two braids and tied the ends with pieces of string. Balamani gave her a mirror, and she smiled as she looked at herself.

"See what a beautiful jewel you are," I said. "Did you know that's what your name means?"

Meena's grin got wider as she moved the mirror to see her hair better.

After our lunch, Balamani had a nap. Meena sat beside me on the veranda, watching as I wrote in my notebook.

"Would you like to learn to write your name, Meena?"

"Can I really do that?" she asked.

"Of course you can." I drew the Telugu symbols for "mee" and "na" and showed her how to make them. I gave her a pencil and a piece of paper from my notebook. From the way she gripped the pencil so tightly, I guessed she'd never held one before. I thought of a better way to start her writing.

"Meena, let's play a game in the dirt. We each need a stick to write with." She found two sticks, and we drew shapes in the dirt in the yard. We took turns copying each other, and soon she was copying the symbols for her name.

"See, you've just made your name! Now do it some more and then you can write it with the pencil." Meena did as I suggested and was delighted when she'd written her name on the paper. She asked me to write the symbols for my name and then for many different words.

My sister came out to sit with us. Meena proudly showed her what she'd learned.

"Do you know how to write, Balamani?"

My sister nodded. "I went to school in my village for a few years before I got married."

"Can you show me after Shanti goes home?" Meena asked.

"I think I can do that," Balamani said. "Would some of your friends like to learn too?"

Meena didn't answer right away. Maybe she liked knowing something the others didn't and wasn't sure about sharing her new skill.

One of the neighbours came into the yard and asked if I'd write a letter for her. It was a short letter, and I finished it quickly. After she'd left, I said, "Balamani, I'm sure some of the women would like to learn to write. Maybe you could have a little class, and Meena could be your helper."

Meena looked excited but my sister said, "I'm not smart like you, Shanti. I couldn't teach anything to the women."

"I think you would be a wonderful teacher," I declared.

Balamani smiled. "We'd better start preparing supper, or they won't be pleased with us."

Meena helped me pick some vegetables from the garden. We chopped them into small pieces for the stew.

While Balamani prepared the meal, she told me about the balika sangha in her village. "There's a meeting tonight. You can come with me," she said. "We talk about our rights and try to help any girl who asks for our support."

"Your mother-in-law allows you to go to the meetings?" I asked, surprised.

Balamani nodded. "She's a member of the women's sangha that started last year. They've been learning about women's rights, and she helped set up our group."

I felt a little nervous about going to a meeting where I'd be the only stranger, but I was curious too. I told my sister I would go with her.

Chapter Six

We were clearing up after our supper when Bhanu said, "I'll finish up here. You girls go on to the balika sangha meeting."

I wondered if my mother would be so eager to have her daughters go to a group. I knew my grandmother would disapprove strongly, saying girls should do as they're told.

On our way to the house where the meeting would be held, two girls joined us and asked me questions. Several girls were chatting in the yard outside the house. They stopped talking and stared at me. I wished I hadn't come, but Balamani took my hand. "This is my sister, Shanti, who is visiting me for a few days. There's no balika sangha in her village. I told her to come to our meeting."

A tall girl wearing a blue salwar kameez came over to us. "I'm Abhaya, the leader of our group. You're welcome to join us." She motioned to the others. "Come inside, all of you. We'll start in a few minutes."

I left my sandals on the veranda and followed Balamani into the house. I sat beside her on a straw mat and looked around the room. There were several posters on the walls, one urging girls to get a good education, another against child marriage, and some showing the importance of sanitation and building latrines.

Abhaya clapped her hands to get everyone's attention. "We're happy to have a guest at our meeting tonight, Balamani's sister, Shanti." I was uncomfortable being pointed out, but I smiled at her.

"Last meeting we discussed Raka's problem. She had to give up school because her family didn't have money for bus fare to go to school in town. Her father said she'd have to stay home and work in the fields," Abhaya said. "Raka, tell us what happened."

The girl sitting across from me sat up straighter and grinned. "I talked to the headmaster at my school, and he spoke with the UNICEF fieldworkers. They will give me money every month for the bus fare and school expenses. So my father agreed I can stay in school." All the girls clapped and cheered.

Balamani nudged me and whispered in my ear, "Maybe you can try that, Shanti." I nodded.

"Raka told me you all gave her courage to talk to her headmaster and not accept her father's decision," Abhaya said.

Raka nodded firmly. "I couldn't have done it without your help. I'm glad we have a sangha."

Abhaya reached to hold a hand of the girl sitting beside her. "Now Prama will tell us her problem. Think about how we can help." She smiled at Prama, who sniffled and wiped her eyes with an end of her scarf.

"My father told me last night he has arranged for me to be married to his cousin whose wife died," she said slowly.

I put my hand over my mouth to cover my gasp. Balamani slid her hand over mine and gently squeezed it. We looked at each other and then at Prama. She didn't look much older than me, and yet her father had already found a husband for her.

Prama looked like she was trying not to cry. "I pleaded with him to let me stay in school. He said he'd beat me if I caused any trouble."

Abhaya put her arm around the girl and looked at the others. "What suggestions do you girls have to help Prama with her big problem?"

Raka pointed to the poster of a child bride with an older man. "We know it's against the law to allow a girl to be married before she's eighteen years old. There are big fines for breaking the law." She said to Prama, "Your father must know the law."

Prama shrugged. "The police never come to our village."

Another girl said, "If we tell the UNICEF worker, she can go to the police in town."

"We've been practicing our Kalajatha on stopping child marriage," Raka said. "When we perform it, Prama could make sure her father sees it."

I remembered seeing a folk drama on education in our village, and I wanted to see this group's Kalajatha drama. I listened carefully as they discussed what they could do for Prama, wondering if some of their suggestions would help me with my father. Finally Abhaya clapped her hands for attention. "You have many good ideas. We need to hear what Prama wants to do."

Everyone looked at Prama, who looked more confident now. She said the best idea was for the UNICEF worker and the girls to go as a group to speak with her father.

Abhaya agreed to talk with the worker. Then she asked what else the girls wanted to discuss, and they talked about how to improve the sanitation in their village.

After that the girls practiced the drama about a girl refusing to be married. As I watched, Balamani told me, "We're going to present this in the village centre soon. We want everyone to know how important it is to stop child marriage."

"I wish our father could see this," I said. I planned to write the actors' words in my book so I could tell my friends at home about it.

After the practice it was time for fun, and we sang some songs and learned a dance Raka showed us.

Although I felt shy talking to Abhaya, I wanted to know how to get a balika sangha in my village. She told me to talk with Deepama, who could contact the women who organize the groups.

As my sister and I walked back to her house, my feelings were a jumble of excitement and worry. "Balamani, I've got to start a sangha in my village. Then I'd have help getting Father to let me go to school."

Balamani sighed. "I know you'll find people to help you soon, Shanti."

During the following days, I continued to help my sister with the chores and tending the garden. When

I wasn't working, I wrote what I could remember of the Kalajatha and added words of my own. Balamani and I had fun acting it out, and Meena loved playing a part in it too.

I also showed Meena more symbols and how to write many words. She was very excited when I gave her some paper and one of my pencils to keep. Several women asked me to write letters for them, and I told them Balamani could write for them as well.

By the end of my visit, I knew I didn't want a life like my sister's, doing household chores and working in the fields. I was more determined than ever to stay in school so I could be a teacher someday.

Chapter Seven

It was hard to say goodbye to Balamani when Deepama came for me. My sister hugged me and said, "I wish you could stay longer. It's been so wonderful having you here."

"I see Shanti has been good medicine for you," Deepama said, smiling.

I felt pleased with their words. I was eager to return to my home and see Mother and my little sister, though I could feel a knot in my stomach thinking about talking with my father.

As I walked with Deepama on the path between fields of rice, we talked about the sangha meeting. I said I'd written all the parts for a drama that the girls could perform in our village. I asked if she could help get a sangha in my village.

"I'm glad you went to the meeting, Shanti," she said. "Tomorrow I will see the people who organize these sanghas. I'll tell them of the need for a group in your village and that one girl is eager to help."

Deepama asked what I did during my days with Balamani. I told her about writing letters for some women and showing Meena how to write her name. She was pleased to hear I'd helped Meena wash her hair. She said she often spoke with villagers about the importance of cleanliness.

"I'm always pleased to hear a family has built a latrine behind their house," she said. "It helps prevent illness." As we talked I wondered how I could convince Father to build our own latrine so we wouldn't have to go to the field at night.

My mother was sweeping the front yard when we arrived. The baby was held close to her chest with one end of her sari. I laid my bundle of clothes on the veranda and put my arms around them both. Deepama checked my sister to be sure she was doing well and then left to visit others in the village.

"How is Balamani?" Mother asked.

"She was sad to see me leave, but she said she felt much better." I held the baby and gently rocked her. "She wants to see our little sister and asked when her naming ceremony will be. Has Father talked with the priest yet?"

Mother nodded. "They chose a date in a few weeks."

"Did the priest tell you what her name should be?"

"Your father didn't say." She pointed toward the path to the well. "There's Danya with water for us. She's been very helpful." Mother took the baby from me to feed her.

As soon as Danya set the water pot down, I hugged her. She grabbed both of my hands and danced around. "In two more days we'll return to school!"

I hoped Mother would say my father had agreed I could go. But she didn't look at me. "Danya, first I have to get my father's permission. I've been thinking of what I can say to him." I took a deep breath and let it out slowly. "He's so determined to do things his way."

My mother didn't say anything. She went into our house. I pulled Danya close to me and whispered, "Tonight I have to talk with Father about returning to school. I don't know whether to weep and plead, or give strong reasons, or try to charm him into letting me go."

Danya smiled. "If you're too charming, he'll think he should get you married. What about showing him what you've learned, like that math test you did well on?"

I shook my head. "Not a test. But I could show him the essay I wrote about education being the key to change and progress."

"You got the top mark for that essay," Danya said. "Tell him that. I must go and help my mother. I'll see you later." She squeezed my hand and ran off.

I picked up the full pot of water and carried it to the backyard. After putting my things away, I asked my mother about preparing our meal. I picked vegetables from our garden and decided I'd weed it before my father came home. I chopped onions and carrots and then started grinding spices to add to the vegetable stew.

My mother squatted beside me while the baby sucked steadily on her breast. She asked about Balamani's house and her in-laws. I told her we'd gone to the balika sangha meeting. When I told how the girls helped Raka and Prama, she put her hand on my arm.

"Shanti, don't speak of that in your father's hearing. He would be angry to hear of girls going against their fathers."

"But the fathers were keeping them from their right to education," I said.

"I know you're hoping your father will allow you to return to school," my mother said. "I wish I could help you, but he's so stubborn when he's made up his mind."

"Did he talk about it when I was away at Balamani's?"

She shook her head. "You'll be happy to know he's showing interest in the baby and even sang to her when I put her in his arms."

"That's good. Maybe he'll forgive her for being a girl."

My mother nudged me and scolded, "Tch! Shanti!" She gave me the baby, and I was happy to hold her, but I was still worried about confronting my father.

The sun was setting when my father and grandmother came down the path. I'd done my best to tidy the room, and the spicy stew smelled good.

"Ah, Shanti, you have returned," my father said as he entered. "How is Balamani?"

I put my palms together in greeting. "Namaste, Father. Namaste, Grandmother. Balamani is getting stronger. She sends you love and hopes she can see you soon."

He grunted in reply as he went through to the backyard to wash. My grandmother followed him. When she returned, she lay on a mat to rest.

My father sat on the other mat, and I brought him his meal. I watched from the cooking place, and when he'd finished, I gave him tea. I'd put a little extra sugar in it. My mother and grandmother came into the room carrying their plates of food and sat opposite him on the other mat. I prayed they would take my side rather than my father's.

"Father, please could I talk with you about school?"

He closed his eyes and sighed loudly. He opened them and looked at me. "What about school?"

"Tomorrow is the last day of our holidays. Our teachers are expecting us for the new term. Danya is returning the next day. She is going with her grandfather on his cart. May I please go with them?"

"I said you'll stay home. Why do you keep asking me about school?"

"Father, my teachers say I am doing very well. I got the top mark for this essay I wrote." I held out my essay to him.

"What did you write about?" he asked, without taking the papers.

"I wrote about education being the key to change and progress."

"Our village needs progress. If you get an education, you will leave and go to the city. How will that help us?"

"Father, I want to help my family and my village. I started our vegetable garden with seeds from our garden at school. Our teachers show us everything about growing things. You have better meals than others in the village because of the vegetables we grow in our yard." I watched his face to see if my words were making him think about changing his mind.

"So you should stay home and tend your garden," he said.

I had to think fast. My argument wasn't going as I hoped. I glanced at my grandmother. "Grandmother is pleased with the garden. I heard her telling her friends about it. She likes looking after it."

My father raised his eyebrows and glanced at his mother. "I suppose you'll tell me she likes milking the goat too."

"She's glad to have milk for yogurt every day." Turning to my grandmother, I said, "Isn't that true?" She frowned at me but tipped her head to each shoulder to show her agreement.

My father shook his head. "Your grandmother also works in the fields. You will stay here and do the chores and prepare for marriage. I told you I will find a suitable husband for you." He looked at me. "I have spoken with a fine man and his father about meeting you."

I opened my mouth to protest, but Father glared

at me and raised his hand. "Say no more. The meeting is arranged," he said firmly. "It will take place tomorrow."

I felt like I was sinking into a muddy pond. I looked at my mother and grandmother, desperate for them to speak. But they both turned away from me and said nothing.

"Go and do your chores," my father said, waving me away as though I was a pesky fly. Then he got up and went outside. The conversation was over.

Chapter Eight

I was too stunned to speak or even cry. My father had never been so angry with me. Although he hadn't touched me, I felt crushed. He didn't seem to care about me at all.

My grandmother carried the plates to the back-yard for washing. Mother knelt in front of me and lifted my chin so our eyes met. "Shanti, I'm sorry I couldn't say anything to help you. When your father decides something, it's hard to change his mind. Maybe tomorrow . . ."

I knew my mother wouldn't go against my father's demands. I thought of Prama at the balika sangha meeting. She wasn't going to give in to her father's plans for her.

"Mother, I'll do my work and then go for water," I said, standing up. I needed to talk with Danya. After cleaning the plates and cooking pot, I got the water pot and hurried down the path. Danya was on her veranda.

"Come with me to the well, now," I pleaded.

"What happened?" she asked, frowning. "Won't your father let you go to school?"

"Just get your water pot and come." As soon as I could speak without others hearing, I told Danya, "Tomorrow my father is meeting with someone he might choose for my husband!"

"Oh no, Shanti! What are you going to do?"

I shook my head. "He doesn't care about me getting an education." I told her about Prama at the sangha meeting and remembered one of the posters and what other girls said about child marriage. "Danya, it's against the law to allow girls to be married before eighteen," I shouted.

Two women we were passing stared at me.

"Not so loud, Shanti," Danya said. "We all know that. But most women in this village, even our own mothers, were married young. No one cares about that."

"Well, I do! And in other villages people are getting the police to stop marriages of girls. Maybe if I tell my father about that—"

I stopped talking, as we'd arrived at the well. Trupti was talking loudly to Sameera about preparations for her marriage while they filled their pots. Danya rolled her eyes at me as we stood waiting for our turn to use the bucket.

Trupti paused in her description of the jewellery she'd wear and looked at us. "Did you two hear that Sameera is getting married? You'll probably be next, Shanti."

I glared at her and turned to Sameera. She was a little older than me, but no more than fifteen. She looked very sad, and I wanted to ask her how she felt but not when Trupti was close by.

Danya and I filled our pots and left. When we were far enough away, I whispered, "Sameera is at least three years below the legal age for marriage. We've got to stop this happening in our village!"

"Trupti says she wants to get married," Danya said.

"But I'm sure Sameera doesn't. Her sister Jyoti was married when she was fourteen, and now she has a baby."

Danya said, "She wouldn't dare say no to her father. He scares me. I heard him yelling at his wife." We'd come to Danya's house, and she turned to go in. "Shanti, be careful. Maybe you shouldn't say any more to your father."

"But I can't just let him ruin my life!"

Danya's mother called to her to come inside. "I'll

see you tomorrow, Shanti," Danya said, leaving me standing on the path.

If my best friend wouldn't help me, maybe I'd just give up and be an obedient daughter. I trudged home, my feelings a confusing mixture of sadness and anger and worry. My bare feet didn't make a sound on the path. I heard low voices coming from my house. I moved silently into the shadows beside the doorway. I lifted the pot off my head and carefully placed it beside me.

"Shanti is doing so well in her studies," my mother said. "Would you allow her to continue another year?"

"There is no need for her to go to school any longer," my father declared. "The dowry for an educated girl is higher. Even now I will have to borrow to pay the dowry they demand."

"School is a waste of her time," my grandmother said. "A man doesn't care about a wife who writes essays. It's more important to cook a good meal and keep a clean house." She went on talking about traditions in the village.

I held my breath and didn't move, trying to decide what to do. Was it best to go inside and interrupt them, or better to go around to the back and pretend I heard nothing? Maybe if they heard me coming they'd stop talking. My father sounded angry, and I didn't want to hear any more from him.

I put the pot on my head and went back on the path a few paces. I sang a favourite tune and walked around the house, then hummed the tune as I poured water into the large pot. I sat on the ground by the doorway, leaning against the cool mud wall. Stars were appearing in the indigo sky, and I wished on the brightest one that I'd return to school.

"Shanti?" My mother squatted beside me. "I heard you singing and thought you were back here. Come inside."

"I can't, Mother. I don't want to listen to Father."

"He just left," my mother said. "If you're asleep before he returns, he won't wake you." She sighed. "Did you hear what he said when I asked if you could continue in school?"

"Yes. Oh, Mother, I don't know what to do!" I sobbed, tears streaming down my face.

My mother held me and rubbed my back. "Come inside and go to sleep. We can talk about it in the morning."

I didn't resist as Mother pulled me up and led me into the house. My grandmother glared at me. I turned toward the wall and pushed all thoughts away, remembering only the starry sky.

Chapter Nine

Mother gently shook my shoulder. "Come, Shanti, we're going to the field before it's light."

I stumbled after her and my grandmother, rubbing my eyes and yawning. I hoped no one would say anything about the talk the day before. I needed time to think about my options and make a plan.

When we returned to our house, I helped prepare breakfast. I avoided my father by milking our goat and looking after the chickens. But when he called me to bring his tea, I had to obey.

"Shanti, I have invited a young man and his parents to come here tonight to meet you and discuss a marriage proposal. You will prepare food to serve them and make a good impression."

I pressed my lips together and kept my head bowed.

"Do you hear me, Shanti?" he said loudly. "Answer me!"

"Yes, Father, I hear you," I murmured.

"Good. Do what your mother tells you to prepare for this."

"Yes, Father." I knew it was best not to say anything about school. Maybe if my father was pleased with me at this meeting, he would listen to my reasons for going to school.

As soon as he and my grandmother left to work in the fields, I asked my mother, "What can I prepare to serve tonight? What else must I do to be ready?"

She told me I should clean the inside of the house, sweep the front yard, draw a *muggulu* design at the entrance, and make two things to serve, one sweet, one savoury. I must bathe and wash my hair. I also had the usual daily chores to do.

After a few hours of sweeping and cleaning, I needed to get out of the house. I made a bundle of the clothes to be washed. "I'm taking the washing to the river," I told my mother.

"Don't be too long," Mother said. "There are many things you must do to prepare for tonight."

I hurried down the path to Danya's house and asked her to come with me. I told her my father had invited the people to our house.

"Oh, Shanti, what will you do?" she said, gathering clothes to wash.

"Help me think of things to make them reject me," I said. "I could make the food taste awful, or I could be clumsy and spill tea on them."

Danya started to giggle. "You could put a cockroach in the food or sing an awful song."

As we walked to the river, we took turns suggesting ideas, each one sillier than the last. I laughed so much I could barely speak.

"I'd like to do all those things," I said, "but my father would be so angry he'd disown me."

"Then you could live with me and go to school," Danya said, grinning.

Speaking of school reminded me of my father refusing to let me go. All my angry feelings drowned my laughter. I slapped a soiled cloth on a flat rock. "No chance of that," I replied. "I'll just have to pretend I'm a dull, obedient girl."

"That'll take some good acting," Danya said.

I finished the washing in silence and spread the clothes on the grass to dry. Danya had more washing to do, so I left her and trudged home.

By midafternoon I had completed most of the tasks and made the food I was to serve. Mother asked me to put my baby sister in the sari hammock on our veranda for a nap. As I sang a lullaby and gently swung the hammock, I planned the muggulu design. When my sister was asleep, I drew my design on the floor at the entrance and filled in the outline with rice flour. It was fun to make muggulu designs for festivals and special celebrations but not for unwelcome visitors. I was concentrating on sprinkling the rice flour in the centre of the design when I realized someone was standing near me.

"Namaste, Shanti." I looked up at Deepama and an older woman I didn't know. "We didn't want to disturb you in the middle of making your beautiful design. This is Bharati. She is in charge of the balika sanghas."

I stood up to greet them. Bharati's warm smile gave me hope that I might get help with my desire for school.

"Do you make a new design each day, or is this for a special occasion?" Bharati asked.

I hesitated, not sure what to tell this woman. "We are having visitors tonight." I didn't look at Deepama, but she probably guessed who the visitors were.

"Deepama told me you are eager to have a sangha here. Usually we start the balika sanghas in villages where there is already a women's sangha. Would your mother be interested in such a group?"

"She's in the back," I said. "I'll get her. Please come in."

The women carefully walked around my design and left their sandals at the door. They followed me into our house, and I unrolled a mat for them to sit on. I went to the backyard and said to my mother, "We have visitors, Deepama and Bharati, a woman from the town who wants to ask you about starting a sangha for the women in our village."

Mother looked puzzled. "Did you invite them in?"

"Yes, Mother, come inside."

She greeted the women. Deepama asked how she was feeling and if the baby continued to feed well. My mother replied all was well. She twisted her hands nervously. I sat down beside her and held her hand.

"Bharati came with me today because I told her Shanti wants to have a balika sangha in the village," Deepama said. "She wonders if you and other women would like to have a sangha as well. I know several of your neighbours are interested."

"I know nothing about these groups," my mother said. "Only what Shanti told me of the one she visited in my older daughter's village."

"There are sanghas in many villages," Bharati said. "The women meet every two weeks to support and help each other. They plan improvements to their community, like growing vegetable gardens."

"My husband would not approve," my mother

said hesitantly. "And my mother-in-law . . ." She shook her head.

"In the beginning there may be challenges," Bharati said. "In other villages, when the older women and the men see how the women in the sangha improve the village, they are very pleased."

I was feeling impatient with this talk. I wanted to get a balika sangha started right away, to help me. "Can we have a girls' sangha if there is no women's sangha?"

Bharati nodded slowly. "It has happened in some villages. It's better when there is support from the girls' mothers." She smiled. "I see your eagerness to get a group here."

I couldn't hold back any longer, and I felt this woman would understand. "There are many girls getting married several years before they're eighteen," I said. My mother squeezed my hand, probably hoping I'd be quiet. But I continued, "We need help to stop this happening."

Bharati raised her eyebrows and looked at Deepama. As I took a breath to continue speaking, my mother squeezed my hand harder, but I was determined to show Bharati how badly we needed a sangha. "At the meeting in my sister's village, a girl said her father planned to have her married. Girls here are afraid to say anything against traditions. Some don't even know what their rights are." I pulled my hand free from Mother's. "Please, can you start a sangha here, very soon?"

Bharati smiled at me. "I will do my best. You can help by talking with girls and getting them to come to a meeting."

"When can we meet?" I asked. "Where?"

"Deepama suggests we meet in the school, if the authorities agree. We will go now and ask." Bharati said to my mother, "I will be happy to help the women organize a sangha as well."

Deepama named women she thought would be interested and encouraged my mother to consider it. Mother bowed her head and was silent. I knew she was afraid of my father's reaction to her joining a group. She might not even agree that I could go to a meeting.

My baby sister started crying, and we all stood up. Mother lifted her out of the hammock.

"She is a lovely baby," Bharati said, smiling as she gently touched my sister's cheek. She and Deepama left after assuring me they'd let me know about a meeting.

As my mother fed the baby, she said, "Shanti, you must not speak of these sanghas to your father. If he learns you asked to start them, he will be angry, I'm sure."

I tried to control my anger, at my father of course, but also at my mother for letting him control her life. "Yes, Mother," was all I dared to say.

I wanted to scream, but it wouldn't help. I went to the backyard and took out my anger pounding spices for our meal.

Chapter Ten

By the time my father and grandmother returned from the fields, a tangled mixture of feelings swirled inside me. Anger at my father simmered under excitement about a balika sangha starting in our village. On top of that was fear and worry about the people coming to my house that evening.

As I served my father supper, I managed to act like an obedient daughter. I put on my plain brown salwar kameez for the meeting and ignored my grandmother's comments that it wasn't my best one. I refused to wear my favourite blue one that looked much better on me.

After we'd cleaned up the supper things, I arranged the food I'd prepared on a tray and prepared the tea. My grandmother was watching for the arrival of the visitors.

"They're coming," she announced as she moved away from the doorway. "Remember everything I told you, Shanti," she said, shaking her finger at me.

My father told me to stand at the back door beside my mother. I could see the father, followed by his son who was a few years older than me, and the mother behind him. Their feet smudged my muggulu design, and they didn't even notice it. I was glad I hadn't spent much time on it.

They entered our house and sat down on our best mat, the parents on either side of their son. My father introduced my grandmother first, as the elder in charge. He beckoned my mother and me forward. "This is my wife, and my lovely daughter, Shanti."

My grandmother had made me practice a proper greeting. I tilted my head slightly and stared at the floor, trying to show that I wasn't interested.

My father told me to bring tea. I was tempted to put some pepper or chili powder in their tea, but I didn't dare. I almost started giggling, remembering the fun Danya and I had talking about what I could do to make the food taste bad.

My baby sister started to whimper, and my father motioned for me to take her outside. I carried her to the backyard and whispered, "Thank you, little one, for getting us out here, away from them. They can talk all they want. I won't let them plan my life."

I was tempted to stay near the doorway and listen, but instead I stood in the shadows where I could watch them. I couldn't imagine living with those people. The son looked grouchy and bored, and his parents argued with loud voices. Surely my father would see it was ridiculous to consider discussing marriage with them. And the whole idea was so wrong.

After a while my mother came outside. She took my sister from me and said, "Shanti, your father wants you to go in. They will ask you some questions. Answer politely."

"Mother, this is all so foolish. Father must see these people are just wanting the dowry and a servant to order around."

"Shh." Mother put her hand on my mouth so I wouldn't say more. "Don't do anything to anger your father or bring shame on our family." She gripped my arm. "*Please*, Shanti."

I turned from her and went inside.

"Sit here," my father said, patting the mat beside him. "I told them your grandmother and mother have taught you well in making meals and keeping a house clean."

"Tell me how you make a vegetable stew," the wife demanded.

I was surprised at the question, but it was easy to answer. Staring at the floor, I slowly listed the steps and only basic ingredients. My grandmother would be annoyed with my reply, as I left out several things.

"Hm," the woman grunted. She asked more questions about cooking and cleaning, and I answered briefly.

The man cleared his throat and stood up. "That will do. We must return to our village before it gets too dark." His wife and son were getting to their feet.

My father got up and said, "As you wish. Thank you for coming. Namaste."

"Namaste," the others mumbled as they went through the doorway. They put on their sandals. The father picked up their lantern, and they left.

I stayed sitting on the mat, watching them leave. I pressed my lips together to keep from saying anything.

Mother came into the room and my father turned toward us. He crossed his arms and stood there. I glanced at my mother and grandmother who were looking at him, waiting for him to speak.

What was he thinking? He'd probably criticize my behaviour. I'd thought about a reply that wouldn't anger him, though it'd be hard to stay respectful.

Finally he said, "I need to sleep. We will talk about this tomorrow. Shanti, get the sleeping mats ready."

I unrolled the mats and blankets.

I lay awake a long time, wondering what my father would say about the meeting. Did he care so little about me he'd agree to send me off to live with those people? If he said he was going to do that, I'd have to find a way to delay the plans until I could get help from others at a sangha meeting. I'd talk to as many girls as possible about balika sanghas and convince them to come to the first meeting.

I thought of Danya returning to school tomorrow, without me. Tears filled my eyes and trickled down my cheeks.

Chapter Eleven

The next morning I tried to forget my worries while I prepared breakfast and milked the goat. But when I brought my father his tea and bowl of rice, I had to keep my hands from shaking. I wished he would say something about last night, as his silence was worse than hearing whatever he might say. I didn't dare to speak first, so I set the tea down carefully and backed away slowly, watching his face.

He cleared his throat and coughed.

"Yes, Father?" I said in a small voice, acting as though he'd spoken.

He looked at me and grunted as he shook his head. "I will talk with your grandmother about my plans for you, and tonight I will tell you."

"Yes, Father," I murmured, surprised and confused by his words. Did he mean his plan to have me married? Or did he have some other plan? Maybe my mother would tell me something when the others left for work. I looked at her but she shrugged her shoulders and shook her head slightly.

As soon as my father and grandmother left the house, I asked Mother, "Do you know what Father is talking about?"

"No, he said nothing to me."

I picked up the water pot. "I'll be back soon. I want to see Danya before she leaves for school." I left before she could reply and got to Danya's house as she was coming out, carrying her bundle of clothes and her school bag.

"Shanti, my grandfather is taking me to town, and he's leaving now. I was hoping you'd come before I left." She looked away. I knew she felt sad that I couldn't return with her.

"I'll walk with you," I said, taking her bundle.

"What happened last night? What did you think of them?" she asked. "I saw them going past my house."

"Oh, Danya, it's all so crazy!" I blurted. "Nothing much happened. I served them tea and the food and didn't dump it on them as I wanted to."

Danya looked shocked, then she grinned.

I sighed. "My father sent me to the backyard with my baby sister so I didn't hear what they said. Then he called me back, and the mother asked me about cooking and cleaning, like a test. I tried not to impress her with my answers."

"Did she seem nice?"

I wrinkled my nose. "She just wants a servant."

"What about her son? Did he speak?"

"Not to me. He sat like a lump of dough and stuffed the food into his mouth."

"And your father? What did he say to you?"

I shook my head. "He said he'll tell me tonight what he's planning. I don't know what he means."

Danya's grandfather was waiting by his ox cart, which was loaded with hay.

"Maybe I can hide in the hay and escape," I said to Danya.

She looked at me with wide eyes, as though I'd really do that. "Oh, Shanti, you know that wouldn't work." She whispered, "I'll tell the schoolmistress why you're not returning, and she'll come and talk with your parents. She did that with other girls who didn't come back, and it worked."

I sighed. "My father won't listen to anyone."

"Come, Danya," her grandfather said. "Time to go."

Danya hugged me and climbed up beside him. I waved and turned around so she wouldn't see my tears. I hurried home.

I did everything Mother asked me to do, trying not to think of anything. The messed up muggulu design reminded me of the visitors, so I grabbed a broom and swept it away. I decided to start talking with the girls in the village about the balika sangha.

Several girls were at the well, chatting and laughing. I felt shy to talk of the meeting, but seeing Sameera made me determined to speak up.

Trupti arrived just then and shouted above the others' chatter, "Shanti, tell us about your marriage plans." All the girls turned and stared at me.

I was about to argue with her, but one look at Sameera made me stop. "I have other plans, Trupti. Come to a balika sangha meeting and learn about your rights." I looked at each of the other girls. "All of you are welcome to come to the first meeting. And bring your friends."

"What else happens at a meeting?" Trupti asked.

"Come and find out," I replied. I placed my water pot on my head and turned to walk home. On the way I met Deepama.

"Shanti, we arranged to hold a meeting at the school the day after tomorrow," she said. "Bharati is coming, and she's bringing Abhaya, the leader of the group in your sister's village. Bharati wants to meet with you in the afternoon to ask what the girls in your village are interested in. Have you spoken to your friends?"

"I just told several girls at the well, and now that I know when we're meeting, I'll tell more girls." I hesitated and bit my lip.

Deepama put her hand on my arm. "Shanti, is there something you want to say to me?"

I made circles in the dust with my toes. "The visitors at our house last night came to see if I'd be a suitable wife." I looked at her. "Oh, Deepama, my father is trying to get me married. I really need the sangha to help me stop him."

Deepama squeezed my shoulders. "Shanti, we will find a way to get you back to school. Try not to worry."

I hurried home and told my mother about the meeting. She twisted the end of her sari. "When your father finds out—"

"He doesn't need to know about it yet," I said, interrupting her. "Please don't say anything, Mother."

In the afternoon I spoke to every girl I saw who was twelve years or older. I told them what the girls talked about at the sangha meeting in Balamani's village. I asked what they'd like to discuss, and some wanted to know more about child marriage. Others were more interested in getting latrines built and cleaning up the village.

"Trupti says you're making trouble for us," one girl said.

"She's afraid she'll miss out on the fun. She's just trying to scare you," I replied.

"What fun?" a younger girl asked. I told them about the dancing and the Kalajatha drama I saw at the meeting. Some of the girls were excited about a sangha, and others were sure their father or mother would forbid them to come.

By the time my father came home, I'd decided not to worry about what he'd say. I felt sure the sangha would help with my problem, and the meeting would be in two days.

When my father finished his supper, I gave him his tea. He frowned. "Shanti, sit down and listen to me." He cleared his throat and glanced at my grandmother, who had started eating. I sat beside her.

"Your grandmother and I were not pleased with your behaviour last night. She said your answers to the questions did not show you are a good cook. They will think you have not been trained well." He glared at me. "You will have another chance to show you would be a good wife."

I gasped and clasped my hands together to keep them from covering my ears.

"Next week you will meet another prospect, much better than the one last night. I expect you to present yourself as your grandmother tells you."

I was silent and didn't move.

"Do you understand, Shanti?" he demanded.

I nodded my head. He picked up his tea and went outside.

My mother set my plate of rice and stew in front of me and sat beside me with her supper. No one spoke as we ate.

There was nothing to say.

Chapter Twelve

The next two days went by quickly. My mother went to work in the fields again. I was busy cleaning and cooking, looking after the garden, and caring for my baby sister. I tried not to think of Danya and what I was missing at school.

In the afternoon before the sangha meeting, Deepama came to my house with Bharati and Abhaya. I greeted them and invited them inside. They told me the plan for the meeting, and we talked about what the girls were interested in discussing.

Soon after they left, my mother returned. "I'm so excited about this meeting," I told her. "I hope lots of girls come."

"Shanti, some of the women said their daughters are going. One woman is afraid her daughter will refuse to stay home and look after the younger children. Another is angry that outsiders are giving girls modern ideas," my mother said. "They didn't know you had started this, and I didn't tell them."

"Oh, Mother, having a sangha will be a good thing for our village."

She sighed. "Your father would not agree with you."

My grandmother came into the house just then, followed not long after by my father. It was hard to act like nothing special was happening while I served my father and grandmother their supper.

On my way to the school for the meeting, I went past the well. Sameera and three girls were there talking.

"The meeting is starting in a few minutes," I said. "Come, all of you, and bring any girls you see."

Sameera hesitated and turned away. I gently took her hand and said, "Come with me now, Sameera."

"I don't think I should," she said slowly, looking at her sister, Jyoti.

"Please come. You'll have fun." One of the girls with her was Manika, who was older than me. She always looked happy, and she was friendly with everyone. "Manika, you're coming, aren't you?"

Manika put her water pot on her head. "I'll take this home first, and then I'll be there."

Sameera and the other two walked with me to

the school, asking questions about sanghas. I was so relieved to see a group of girls standing outside the school, talking with Deepama. She waved and smiled at us.

"Come inside," she said. "Bharati and Abhaya have everything set up, and some girls are already there."

I saw Trupti talking with Abhaya. She'd probably come because she was curious. She always wanted to be the first to know about anything new in the village. Two of her friends were with her, and they were wearing colourful salwar kameez, glad for an excuse to dress up.

The girls were looking at the same posters on child marriage and sanitation that I'd seen at the balika sangha in Balamani's village. Manika came in with three more girls. Bharati asked everyone to sit on the mats spread on the floor.

"I'm so glad to see you all here," Deepama said. She introduced Bharati and Abhaya, and they told us about balika sanghas. I looked at the girls' faces as Abhaya explained how her friends helped each other stand up for their rights.

"We've had a sangha for three years, and we've stopped eight child marriages," Abhaya said. Trupti stared at her, frowning, and her friends nudged each other.

I glanced at Sameera. Her head was bowed and she twisted the end of her scarf. I noticed that Bharati was also watching the girls' reactions to Abhaya, and I hoped she'd soon talk about the fun part of the meetings.

"You've heard some reasons why we have sanghas," Bharati said. "Abhaya can tell you what the girls say they like about getting together and having a sangha in their village."

Abhaya described several projects that had helped her community, like planting trees and gardens and building latrines.

"What would make your life better in this village?" she asked us. "How could working together in a sangha help you?"

"Having a latrine at my own house," Trupti said. Her friends giggled and nodded in agreement.

"Getting rid of all the garbage everywhere," Manika said.

One girl suggested more vegetable gardens would be good. Another girl said, "I'd like to have water pipes in my yard so I don't have to go the well." Deepama wrote the ideas on the blackboard.

Abhaya remembered I'd seen the Kalajatha and asked me to help her perform part of it. It was fun improvising with her, and the girls applauded us.

Then she said, "The girls in my sangha like to show each other dances they've learned. Would you like to do that?" Most of the girls nodded. "I'll show you one I know. Please join me and then maybe someone has another dance we can do." Soon everyone was dancing and singing, and I noticed that even Trupti looked like she was having a good time.

When we'd settled down on the mats again, Bharati said, "Every sangha has two leaders who plan the meetings and keep everything moving smoothly. Girls who would like to be a leader are asked to write an essay saying why they want to do that and how they think a sangha will help the girls in their village." She looked at me and then at the others. "Who would like to be a leader? Can you suggest someone who would?"

"Manika would be a good leader," one of her friends said. Manika grinned and shrugged. Bharati asked her if she'd like to, and Manika tipped her head in agreement.

The girls near Trupti nudged her and one said her name. But she shook her head firmly. I was relieved, as she'd be bossy and arguing all the time.

"Shanti, what about you?" someone said. I was surprised, as I was one of the younger ones there. But others agreed and Bharati asked me if I'd like to be a leader. I nodded slowly. I liked Manika, and I was sure we'd work well together.

"I would like to be a leader, too," Trupti said loudly. Everyone looked at her.

"Good," Bharati said, and smiled. "Anyone else?" When no others spoke up she said, "You three girls, and any others who would like to be a leader, will write a short essay. Give it to Deepama. We will choose two girls for leaders, and we'll help them plan the next meeting."

She thanked us all for coming and encouraged us to bring friends to the next meeting. Some girls left then and others talked with Abhaya and Bharati.

As I was leaving, Deepama smiled at me. "Shanti, that was a good meeting. You did well getting so many girls to come. Can you stay a little longer?"

"No, I have to go," I said. "Thank you for your help with this." I hurried home, hoping to avoid questions about where I'd been. My father wasn't home when I got there, and my grandmother was on her sleeping mat, snoring softly.

My mother beckoned me into the backyard, and we talked in whispers about the meeting. "Your father asked where you were, and I said you'd gone to see a friend. He said—" she hesitated, looking away from me.

"What did he say?" I demanded.

"He said you must prepare food for a man who's coming tomorrow night to make marriage plans," my mother mumbled. "I didn't want to tell you tonight, but—"

"Oh, Mother," I moaned. My excitement about the sangha was smothered by anger and despair. But then I remembered my right to education and to refuse marriage.

"I'll prepare food and present myself as Father says, but I will not be married until I choose to be."

I went inside, changed into my sleeping clothes, and lay on my mat. I was determined to forget my worry and anger. Instead, I thought about dancing with my friends that night and felt pleased that I helped get a balika sangha in our village.

Chapter Thirteen

The next morning as I gave my father rice and tea, my grandmother said, "Shanti, sit down here and listen to me."

I sat beside her. She held my arm firmly.

"Tonight you will show the visitors you will be a good wife. You can prepare the same food as the last time. You will wear your best salwar kameez. You will answer any questions properly, to show you are a good cook and look after a house well."

"Yes, Grandmother," I murmured.

"No foolishness like you did with that other family." She shook my arm. "Understand?"

I nodded and looked away. I gritted my teeth to keep from yelling out what I really wanted to say.

"Go now and help your mother so she can get to work." She took a sip of tea.

I didn't look at my father as I went to the back-yard. When he and my mother and grandmother had gone, I prepared the food to be served while my baby sister napped. I wanted to write the essay to give to Deepama, but first I hoped to talk with some of the girls who had come to the meeting.

I made a sling from a piece of cloth to hold my baby sister against my chest. She slept as I walked to the well. I heard Trupti's loud voice.

When she saw me she called out, "Shanti, have you written your essay yet? I just gave mine to Deepama."

I almost said, "Who wrote it for you?" as I knew she wrote poorly when she was in school with me. But I just replied, "I'm working on it." The girls gathered around me to see the baby, ignoring Trupti. She turned away and left.

As I waited for a turn with the bucket, I asked the others if they liked the meeting.

"The dancing was so much fun," one girl said, making a few dance moves. "I'll come to every meeting if we get to dance."

"Abhaya is a good dancer," I said. "She's also very good as a sangha leader. She's organized projects to improve her village and helped girls stand up for their rights." I said this directly to Sameera, who had just arrived with her water pot.

One of her friends asked me, "Could our sangha stop Sameera's marriage?"

"At the sangha meeting in my sister's village, I saw Abhaya and the group plan how to help a girl, Prama, refuse to be married," I told them. "Yesterday I asked Abhaya about that. She said the plan was successful, and Prama is going to school. Her parents have promised she can decide when she wants to get married."

The girls murmured and nudged Sameera. The baby was awake and squirming. I filled my water pot. "I have to take my sister to my mother for feeding," I said, then walked away.

I left the pot at my house and went to where my mother was working. After Mother fed the baby, I hurried home. While my sister slept in the hammock, I wrote my essay. I was happy to be writing and wished I could spend all day doing that.

But instead I swept the floors and the yard and started preparations for supper. When Mother returned she said, "You should make a muggulu at the entrance. Your grandmother will be angry if you don't."

"Oh, I'm so tired of trying to please her," I complained. "I'll make a simple design that won't take too long. The other visitors didn't even notice the muggulu."

"They would have noticed if you hadn't made one," my mother said.

I got the rice powder and drew a circle with a mandala inside it.

When my father and grandmother returned from work, Grandmother stepped over the muggulu. "You should have made a much better design, Shanti," she said, shaking her finger. "But that will have to do. There's no time to add more." She lifted the cloth off the tray of food I'd prepared. "This looks good."

She reminded me of how I was to behave and what I should say. "This man's wife died and he has three children. So he'll want to know you can look after them as well as do the cooking and cleaning."

"What? He has children? How old is he?" I asked. I glared at my father for arranging a meeting and not telling me any of this.

"His age is not your concern," my father said. "He has a good job, and he needs a wife. His brother is coming with him to meet you."

"And his mother?" I asked, barely controlling my anger.

"No, she's looking after his children."

I won't have to answer questions about cooking, I thought. *But, three children! And he'll be* old. *Maybe if I act childish he'll see I won't be suitable as a mother. I'd rather be rejected than have to tell my father I refuse to be married.*

After supper, I changed into my blue salwar kameez that my grandmother insisted I wear. I was braiding my hair when Grandmother said, "You look too young. I'll put your braid into a bun." Before I could object, she'd twisted my braid into a tight bun and secured it with pins.

"They're coming," my father said, standing at the doorway. "Shanti, be ready to serve them tea." He went out to welcome them.

Before I went to the back, I saw the two men in our yard. Both were taller than my father and were neatly dressed in long pants and plain coloured shirts.

From the backyard I watched as Father introduced my grandmother to the men, named Daksha and Balraj. The men sat on the mat across from Grandmother. Balraj had some grey hair, so I guessed he was the widower. Both men were nice-looking and spoke quietly and politely.

"Shanti!" my father called. I came to the doorway, and he beckoned me to enter.

The visitors stood up and greeted me with "Namaste," their palms pressed together.

I returned the greeting and then looked into Balraj's dark eyes. He smiled and I had a strange feeling. I looked down.

"Bring in the tea, Shanti," my grandmother said. I backed out of the room. My mother held out a tray with four tumblers of tea. I took it from her, breathed deeply to calm myself, and walked slowly into the room. I was careful not to look at either man. After serving the tea, I returned for the tray of food. As I offered it to the visitors, Balraj asked me what I'd prepared.

"Tell them, Shanti," my grandmother said, as I'd hesitated. I told him what was in the pakora and samosa. Balraj took one of each and murmured his approval when he bit into the samosa.

As I retreated to the yard, I felt confused. Balraj was so different from the other marriage prospect. Although he was much older, he seemed to be nice, and he was handsome. But my mind screamed that I'm too young to be married, and I want to go to school.

My father called me in again and told me to sit beside my grandmother. Balraj asked me, "How long did you go to school?"

"I finished eighth form at our village school, and I went for one term to the high school in town." If he asked why I didn't continue, I'd want to say my father refused to let me return.

But instead Balraj said to my father, "That's

enough education for girls. They don't need more to look after children and a house."

As the other men agreed with him and my grandmother nodded, I wanted to stand up and shout, "You're all wrong!" But I hugged myself tightly instead to keep everything in.

His comment shouldn't have surprised me as he was here to find a wife, but his kind face had fooled me.

Father said, "Shanti, leave us now." He probably wanted me out of the room before I spoke out. I got up and went to the backyard. I took my baby sister from my mother and held her close to me.

"Did you hear that, Mother?" I asked her. "Are men afraid we are smarter than them?"

My mother just shook her head. I paced around the yard so I couldn't hear the talk in the house.

A while later, my father called to us. "They've left. Come inside." As we entered, he said, "We finally agreed on a date for your wedding, Shanti. Balraj wanted it to be in a few weeks, but I said we needed more time to prepare."

I didn't want to hear more. I put my sister in my mother's arms and ran outside and down the path to the field we used for a latrine. At the edge of the field I leaned over and vomited.

My mother came beside me and placed one hand on my forehead, the other on my back. When I stopped retching, she gave me a damp cloth to wipe my face. She held me while I sobbed. I felt so defeated and powerless.

"Oh, Mother, I don't want to go inside the house and hear Father talk about wedding plans."

"No more talk tonight," my mother said, and she led me back home.

Chapter Fourteen

That night I had nightmares about weddings. I was relieved that my father and grandmother didn't talk about wedding plans the next morning before they went to work.

I didn't want to go to the well or anywhere I'd meet other girls. They would already know of the marriage plans, as it's impossible to keep a secret in the village. I was weeding the garden when Deepama came into the yard. She was the only person I did want to see.

"Shanti, I was hoping you'd be home. I heard about your father's plans for your marriage," she said, holding out her arms to me.

"Oh, Deepama, I *can't* marry that man. Will you speak to my father?"

"He won't listen to me," Deepama said. "You can ask for help at the next meeting of your sangha."

"But Trupti wants to be a leader, and she doesn't care about child marriage," I cried. "She won't let anything stop her marriage."

"Trupti is only one voice," Deepama said. "I'm sure when the girls learn more about their rights, and the laws, they'll support you."

"But I need help *now*," I said. "My father's set a date, and my grandmother will start preparations, and—"

"Shanti," Deepama said, holding my shoulders firmly and looking at me. "Calm down. I have a few minutes if you want to talk about how you could present your problem to the girls in the sangha when we meet in a few days."

I had finished my essay about being a leader and how the sangha could help the girls in our village, and I gave it to Deepama. We talked about the girls asking for help at the meeting in Balamani's village, and that helped me plan what to say. When Deepama left, I felt more confident.

I needed to get water to fill our big pot. Maybe most of the girls would be busy inside their homes and I wouldn't have to answer questions about my father's plans. I put my sister in the sling and went to the well. I was glad only Sameera was there.

"Shanti, the girls were talking about the men who

came to your house last night. They said you'll be getting married soon. Is that true?"

I took a deep breath. "Sameera, I don't want to talk where others will hear us. Come back to my house and I'll tell you my plan."

A woman had arrived at the well and was waiting for a turn. I filled my pot and handed the bucket to her. Sameera helped me settle my pot on my head before picking up her own pot. She walked beside me and we chatted about my sister.

As we entered my house, she said, "I can't stay long. I have many chores to do today. But I want to know your plan."

I looked into her eyes and gripped her arm. "Sameera, no one must hear of this before our next meeting. Do you promise not to tell?"

She nodded. "I promise. I'm hoping—" She looked down.

"Sameera, do you want to stop your wedding plans too?"

She nodded, very slowly. "I'm so afraid of what my father will do," she whispered.

"Deepama helped me with my plan, and I know she'll do everything she can to help you too." I told her what I'd say at the meeting. As we talked about how to reply when our families discussed wedding plans, Sameera relaxed a little. When she left to do her chores, I felt much less alone and even more determined to demand our rights.

My sister started whimpering, so I tucked her into the sling and walked toward the rice fields. On my way there, I was surprised to see the schoolmistress from town, Mrs. Das, and another woman waving to me.

"Shanti," Mrs. Das said, "we came to ask your parents to send you back to school. Are they at your house?"

I stood still. I knew my father would be angry to have strangers interfering in his plans.

"This is Kumari from UNICEF. She can offer your parents funds for school," Mrs. Das said. "Where is your father?"

Several neighbours had stopped and were listening. I mumbled, "He's working in the fields. So is my mother."

"Can you take us to them? Or ask them to meet us at your house?"

I couldn't think what was worse, my father shouting where everyone could hear, or his anger at me for bringing strangers to his house. "I'm taking the baby to my mother for feeding," I said. "You can come talk with her."

As we walked, Mrs. Das said Danya told her about my father's plans. When we came to the field where my mother was working, I called her to come. "Mother, these women want to talk with you." I introduced them and we all sat in the shade of a banyan tree. My grandmother and another woman came and stood near us.

"Shanti is a very good student," Mrs. Das said. "I am asking you to let her return to school so she can get a good education."

"Her father decides these things," my mother said. "We can only do as he says."

My grandmother said loudly, "I am Shanti's grandmother. She doesn't need any more education. No one in our village needs education to work in the fields."

Mrs. Das smiled at her. "I'm sure you have helped in raising Shanti to be the wonderful girl she is. Wouldn't you like her to have opportunities you didn't have? Shanti could be a teacher."

My grandmother muttered, "Her father decides about her future."

"Where is Shanti's father?" Mrs. Das asked. I pointed to three men who were loading straw onto an ox cart.

"Would you ask him to meet with us at your house?" Mrs. Das asked.

I nodded and turned to go to the cart.

"Tell him we're waiting for him there," my grandmother said. "Your mother and I will take these women to our house now." They started down the path as I slowly walked to my father.

Two small boys who'd been listening ran ahead of me, and I knew they'd tell my father. I didn't have time to sort my mixture of hopeful and anxious feelings. He was striding toward me.

"What is this, Shanti?" he demanded. "Strangers are telling me to leave my work to talk about you going to school? Who are they? What did you tell them?"

"Father, I'm so sorry. I didn't expect them. Mother and Grandmother told them you make the decisions, and so they want to talk with you. They are waiting at our house now."

"Let's go, then," my father said, walking ahead of me. He was silent during the few minutes it took to get home.

The two boys followed us, and several people were in our yard, all waiting to hear the confrontation. My father shouted, waving them away. They moved from the doorway to let us through, then crowded around again.

"Namaste," my father sternly greeted the visitors.

Mrs. Das and Kumari stood up and said "Namaste" firmly and respectfully. They introduced themselves.

"I was told you came to speak to me about my daughter," Father said.

"That is correct," Mrs. Das said. "I'm asking you to send her back to school, and Kumari is offering funds from UNICEF for school costs." My father glanced at my grandmother. Mrs. Das said, "Shanti is an excellent student, and she deserves the opportunity for an education."

My father said loudly, "We have other plans for Shanti."

"Is it true you are planning her marriage?" Mrs. Das asked. "She is well below the legal age for marriage. You could be charged."

My father looked at his feet. "My daughter is not your concern. She is my responsibility, and I do what is best for her."

"I ask you to think carefully what is truly best for Shanti," Mrs. Das said. "It is not good for any girl to be married young and start having babies."

I watched anxiously as my father took deep breaths and looked as though he'd explode. "Shanti is not returning to school. She is needed here," he said firmly. "Now I must return to work. My mother and my wife must return to work also." He turned and pushed through the crowd at the doorway.

My grandmother said to my mother, "Give the baby to Shanti. Come with me." She glanced at Mrs. Das and Kumari as she said, "Namaste."

Mother put my sleeping sister in my arms. She whispered to the women, "I'm sorry. Thank you for coming. Namaste."

Mrs. Das gently touched my mother's shoulder. "It's good we came. I see that you truly care about Shanti's future. Please send word to me if your husband changes his mind."

My mother nodded and followed my grandmother.

Mrs. Das sighed and shook her head. "I'm sorry, Shanti. I thought your father would agree to let you go when I said he could be charged and when we explained about the UNICEF money." She smiled at me. "But he's thinking about it, and I believe he does care about you. We will keep hoping." She hugged me.

I held back my tears until the women left, then let them flow freely.

Chapter Fifteen

During the next few days I avoided going to the well earlier in the morning when most of the girls went. But one day when I was getting water, Trupti came with another girl. I wished I could disappear.

"Shanti, we heard you're getting married," Trupti said with a grin. "Your grandmother asked my mother about food we're preparing for my wedding. You should come to my house and see my jewellery and new clothes so you'll know what to ask for."

I turned to face her. "Thanks, but I have too many things to do." I wanted to say "more important things" but knew it was better not to offend her. "I have to go," I said, picking up my pot of water.

"But Shanti, we have so much to talk about now," Trupti said. I just waved and kept on walking.

Later that day I went by Manika's house. I hoped

to talk with her, as I was sure she'd be chosen as one of the sangha leaders, and it was important to have her on my side.

"Shanti," she called from her yard where she was washing clothes. Her little brothers chased around her. "Stop for a few minutes so I can see your little sister."

I came closer and moved the sling away from my sister's face. She seemed to be asleep, though when I rubbed her back she burped loudly. Manika grinned and her brothers laughed.

"She's so sweet," Manika murmured, gently stroking the baby's cheek.

"Manika, did you give Deepama your essay?"

She nodded. "It'd be fun if we two are leaders. What projects do you think we'll start working on?"

"I'm sure you'll be chosen," I said. "Manika, has your father ever talked about arranging your marriage?"

"He may have thought about it. But when my mother died two years ago, he needed me to look after my brothers. There aren't any grandmothers to take charge of our house and no relatives who'd take the boys in." She shrugged. "So that was the end of my education. Now I'm used to it, and I don't mind."

I kept my eyes on the design my foot was making

in the dust. "I'm sure you've heard that my father's arranging my marriage. At the next meeting I'm going to ask the girls to help me stop the plan." I looked at her. "Will you help me with that?"

Manika hugged me. "Of course I will. Even though it's the village custom and our mothers and grandmothers were married young, it's not good for us to marry early. And it's illegal."

"I'm so glad you agree. Most of the other girls will follow what you do. Deepama helped me plan what to say, and Sameera said she wants our help too." I put my hand on my mouth. "Please don't tell anyone that. She's so afraid of her father."

A splash and a yell made us turn around. Her younger brother had fallen into the tub of water. Manika lifted him out, soothing him.

She smiled at me. "We'll talk later, Shanti."

"You won't tell—" I started.

She shook her head firmly. "I won't say a word to anyone."

"Thanks, Manika."

My mother came home while I was preparing supper. She sat down near me, leaned against the wall, and closed her eyes.

I brought her a tumbler of water. "Mother, you're so tired. Can't you come home sooner?"

She shook her head. "We need my earnings." The baby started crying, and I brought her to my mother to be fed.

"Shanti, the women working beside me were talking about the balika sangha. They said you girls are going to cause problems. One woman won't allow her daughter to go."

I groaned. "Did you tell them we'll make our village a better place to live?"

Mother looked away from me. "Before I could say anything, another woman asked me when you're getting married."

"What did you say?"

"I said your father was making the plans. Then they wanted to talk about the food, the clothes, the jewellery."

I was silent and stirred the steaming rice. My mother wouldn't be any help in stopping this marriage, even though I was sure she didn't agree with it.

When I served my father and grandmother their supper, I said nothing and returned to the cooking fire, hoping to avoid any talk of the plans.

On the day of the sangha meeting, I saw Manika with her brothers at the pond. We talked about what to tell the girls about helping me stop the marriage plans.

After supper I hurried through cleaning up and walked toward the school. As I came to Sameera's house, she and Jyoti were waiting for me. "Can my sister come to the meeting even though she's married? Our mother will look after her baby."

"Of course she can come," I said. I was surprised but very glad Jyoti was interested. I'd heard she had a difficult time in her marriage.

As we walked, Sameera asked, "Will you be one of the leaders?"

I shook my head. "Bharati said she'd talk with the two girls they chose before the meeting, so I know I'm not one."

When we arrived, Manika and Trupti were helping Deepama and Bharati put up the posters and spread mats in the room we'd use. Manika smiled at me and rolled her eyes toward Trupti. I raised my eyebrows, but she said nothing. I guessed these two were the leaders.

The girls came in twos and threes and soon filled the room. A few mothers had come too, and I heard Bharati tell them this sangha was for the girls. She said the women were welcome to stay, and she asked them to sit on mats at the back of the room.

Manika whispered to me, "Look who just came in." She nodded toward the women. Trupti's mother sauntered to the back of the room and sat beside the other women. I was worried, as she had a reputation in the village for arguing against anything she disagreed with.

Bharati clapped her hands to get everyone's attention. "Please find a place to sit, and we'll start the meeting." As soon as everyone settled, she continued. "Welcome. I'm so glad to see so many here. The two leaders we chose will lead this meeting with me. Manika and Trupti, please come." Everyone clapped as they went to the front.

"First I'll give you some information, then Manika will lead the first part of our meeting. Trupti will lead the dancing and games," Bharati said. Trupti grinned and waved at her friends, enjoying the attention.

After the two girls sat down, Bharati told us about the importance of sanitation for good health. I couldn't concentrate as I was thinking about what I was going to tell the others about my problem.

When Bharati finished, Manika got up and said, "Now it's time for you girls to tell us what you want to talk about." She looked at me as she said the last words, and I raised my hand. "Shanti?"

I stood beside Manika. "My father is planning my marriage, and I need you girls to help me stop this plan so I can return to school."

"How can we help you?" Manika asked.

I looked at several girls. "We know it's against the law for girls to be married before they're eighteen." I pointed to the poster that showed this. "My father doesn't listen when I tell him. Maybe if a group of girls come to my house chanting 'No more child marriage,' he'll pay attention."

I saw Trupti turn around, looking at her mother.

Manika said, "This is a chance to show our village that we girls know our rights and we will support each other in claiming them." She held my hand. "I'll be part of the group going to Shanti's house. Who will join me?"

A few girls raised their hands, and Trupti's mother stood up, shouting, "You girls are causing trouble for our village! We don't want you making a disturbance. That will bring the police, who'll interfere in our customs."

Bharati had quietly moved to the back, and she whispered something to Trupti's mother and led her out of the room. We could hear Trupti's mother arguing loudly outside. A few minutes later Bharati came into the room and stood at the door.

Trupti was shaking her head and hiding her face in her hands. Was she crying or was she going to yell at us? Would she use her role as a leader to stop my plan?

She raised her hand and said quietly, "I'm sorry my mother yelled at us. She's worried you'll try to stop *my* marriage." Trupti sighed and I was surprised to see her eyes had filled with tears. I wondered if she didn't want to be married any more than I did.

Manika looked at me and at Bharati, who motioned for her to continue. Manika said, "Well, Shanti is asking for our help. Let's decide what we'll do."

"I think we should do a Kalajatha in front of her house," one girl suggested. "When Shanti's father comes to watch, we'll go talk with him."

"But we don't know the drama about child marriage," another girl said.

"I've written out all the parts of the one I saw, and I can show you," I said.

"Shanti, do you think a Kalajatha is a good idea?" asked Manika.

I nodded slowly, imagining my father seeing it. "Yes, it might be the best thing."

"We could practice right after the meeting,"

Manika said. "Anyone who wants to be in the drama or help with it can stay for a while."

Manika asked what else the girls wanted to talk about. Several girls suggested projects they'd like to do, such as planting vegetable gardens and building latrines.

When it was Trupti's turn to lead, she was back to her usual bossy and giggly self. She was good at teaching us the moves of a dance she knew well. Everyone was having fun.

Finally Bharati said it was time to end the meeting. She congratulated the leaders for doing so well.

As the girls started to leave, Manika said, "All who want to help with the Kalajatha, come beside me." Several girls gathered around her and others stood by the door, maybe waiting to see what we'd do before joining us. Sameera was with them, and I waved her to come closer. She shook her head and stayed where she was.

I described the main characters in the drama, a girl and her parents, the groom and his parents, the health worker, and a teacher. Everyone else would be friends or neighbours, some saying a few lines.

Manika said, "Shanti, will you play the part of the girl?"

I shook my head firmly. "No. My father would

be so angry. But I could be the health worker who tells the parents that it's dangerous for girls to have babies when they're too young."

One girl suggested Manika would be the best person to be the girl. She agreed, and then several girls volunteered to play the other main parts. I told each person what they should say, and they had fun adding their own lines to make it more dramatic. Manika was very good at organizing us, and we practiced the whole play before it was time to leave. She invited us to come to her house the next evening after supper to practice it.

I left the meeting with Sameera who had stayed to watch us practice. I felt excited about performing the drama and scared about my father's reaction. I knew I had to do everything possible to convince him of my rights. At least now I had the support of my friends.

Chapter Sixteen

Back home, I went quietly into my yard and was startled to see my grandmother standing outside the door.

"You were at that meeting a long time," she scolded, shaking her finger in my face. "The woman next door said she saw you all dancing and singing. You don't have time for such childish things. If your father hears about this, he will forbid you to go to meetings."

I glanced at Mother, lying on her sleeping mat, watching us. Why wasn't she saying anything?

My grandmother grumbled on while I spread out the rest of the mats. I knew it was best to be silent. When we'd both settled on our mats, I thought about how I could go to the practice at Manika's house without my grandmother knowing.

The next day I did extra chores so my grandmother wouldn't complain or think of other tasks I should do. I told Manika about my grandmother when we were at the river washing clothes.

"Come to my house this afternoon to make a sweet," Manika suggested. "If your grandmother asks where you're going after supper, tell her I'm giving you a cooking lesson. Then after our practice you can take her the sweet we've made."

"Thanks, Manika," I said. "That's a good idea. She knows you're a good cook."

That evening after I'd served my father and grandmother the supper I'd made, I heard them talking. Grandmother called to me, "Shanti, these vegetables are very tasty. You've added different spices. What did you do?"

I was pleased to get a compliment from her, and I told her how I'd prepared the vegetables.

She nodded. "It's good you're cooking well. Soon we will start making some of the food for your wedding." I left the room so she wouldn't see the scowl on my face. She said to my father, "I'll need money for supplies to make the sweets and other food for the wedding."

Father groaned. "You'll also be asking for money

to buy Shanti's wedding sari and jewellery. I'll have to borrow from the moneylender."

I wanted to scream at them to stop their plans and save the money. Instead I whispered to my mother, "Can't you tell them this is all wrong?"

Mother put her hand on my mouth. "Don't say anything now. Maybe we can talk with your grandmother after your father goes out with his tea."

I shook my head. "I don't want to talk with her. Give her the baby to hold while we're eating so she won't talk about wedding plans. I'll clean up out here, and then I'm going to Manika's. If she asks where I am, just tell her Manika is teaching me to make some special sweets."

My father called for his tea. I gave him the tea and took his empty plate to the backyard.

As soon as the dishes and pots were washed, I hurried to Manika's house. Most of the girls had arrived, and I was surprised and very glad to see Sameera there. I hugged her. "Sameera, you're so brave to come."

She smiled shyly. "I wanted to be part of this drama. You showed me we have to take a stand for ourselves."

As Manika started the practice, I interrupted. "My father and grandmother are talking seriously about plans for my wedding. Can we do the drama tomorrow evening?"

"We just learned our parts. We can't be ready so soon," one girl protested.

"If we practice hard tonight, I think we can," Sameera said. Everyone looked at her, surprised to hear her speak up. "Shanti needs our help, and we agreed to help her."

After a little more discussion, the girls agreed. I really wished I could just sing in the background instead of having a part as one of the characters trying to convince the family to stop the marriage plans and send the girl back to school. But I'd have to face my father's anger about joining the sangha anyway, so I might as well play a part to show him my determination to demand my rights.

An hour later we'd practiced the drama several times and most of us were feeling confident and excited about performing. Even Sameera was comfortable with her small part as one of the crowd who would be chanting.

I stayed a few minutes after the others left, and Manika gave me a package of the sweets we'd made in the afternoon to take home. I wanted to have something to show my grandmother in case she asked where I'd been that evening.

Chapter Seventeen

The next day I kept thinking about the Kalajatha we would present in the village after supper and wondered how my father would react.

When I took my sister to my mother in the field, one of the women working with her called, "Here comes the beautiful bride! Shanti, we've been telling your mother you're a lucky girl to be chosen for Balraj."

I looked away and bit my lip to keep from saying anything. Mother came to me and we walked away to sit in the shade of a tree.

"Shanti, you did well to ignore that woman."

"Mother, I hope those women see our drama toni—" I didn't mean to tell my mother we were performing that night. I didn't want my father to think she'd talked with me about it.

"You're doing a drama tonight?" my mother asked. "Where?"

"Oh, Mother, I didn't want you to know. Just act surprised when you see us so Father won't be angry with you for not telling him about it." My mother shrugged. "Listen for our singing, and tell him and Grandmother to come outside."

Later in the day I was sweeping the yard when Sameera came by carrying her water pot.

"Trupti came to the well while I was there," she said. "She asked me when the Kalajatha was being performed and said she wanted to join us."

"Did you tell her?" I doubted Trupti could be trusted to be helpful rather than disruptive.

Sameera sighed. "I wished you or Manika were there to answer her. I told her to ask Manika about it. Then I left."

That afternoon I took extra time to prepare one of my father's favourite dishes for supper. Maybe it would help put him in a better mood when he watched the Kalajatha.

As soon as I could get away after supper, I went to Manika's house. Most of the girls in the drama were already there. I asked Manika if Trupti was coming, and she said Trupti decided she'd watch it with her mother to keep her from disrupting the performance.

I had brought my mother's blue cotton sari, and

Sameera helped me dress in it for my role as the health care worker.

"I'll probably trip on the hem," I said. "It's so much easier to move in my salwar kameez."

"You'll be fine, Shanti," Sameera said. "Shall I pin your braid into a bun to make you look older?"

I nodded. "Maybe it'll give me courage, too. I'm really worried about what my father might do when he sees me in this drama."

Manika heard me and grabbed my hand. "Shanti, we're doing this because we girls want everyone to know child marriage must stop. Keep thinking of that. We'll help you with whatever happens later."

I stood straight. "Right. Thanks, Manika."

Some of the girls said they were nervous, although everyone was excited to be performing. Except for the girls playing the parts of the parents, the others wore colourful salwar kameez and anklets with bells. We rehearsed the song we were going to sing when we walked to the space where we'd perform.

Manika grinned. "We sound really good. Let's go!"

She led the way and a girl on either side of her held up a poster about child marriage being illegal. The rest of us followed them, clapping in time to our song. As we walked down the street, people came out of their homes. Some children playing outside marched and danced beside us. One of the girls in our group called out, "Come and see our Kalajatha!"

I enjoyed the fun until we came near my house. My father was sitting on the veranda, and my mother and grandmother stood near him. All three were watching our procession.

Sameera squeezed my hand and I smiled at her, trying to push away my fears. We stopped at the centre of the village, under a banyan tree.

Manika announced, "Please come and watch the first performance of our Kalajatha. We are members of the first balika sangha in our village. Our drama is about girls' rights."

We stood in a semicircle, and Manika and the girls playing the parts of the parents moved to the centre for the first scene. The girl playing the father was very dramatic, telling his fifteen-year-old daughter about the marriage plans. When Manika stamped her foot and shouted, "I won't marry that old man!" the people watching were silent. Then one woman started clapping and others joined in. I glanced at my father. He looked like a statue, sitting with his arms folded across his chest.

I was in the next scene, and I breathed deeply to calm my pounding heart. I spoke clearly the reasons why girls should not be married young. After I said, "Many teenaged girls who have babies die in childbirth," I heard women murmuring to each other. Trupti was standing beside her mother at the edge of the crowd. I hoped she'd keep her mother from yelling at us.

The last scene showed the girl being welcomed back at school. All the girls joined in a joyful dance. The crowd applauded and a few cheered. I noticed my father didn't applaud.

When the drama was finished we sang our song again as we walked back to Manika's house. Deepama was waiting there for us. "You all did very well in the drama, and I heard many people talking about it."

Sameera and I stayed at Manika's house a little longer before going home. I wasn't ready yet to face my father. But I was worried he might be questioning my mother about me, and I didn't want her to have to defend me or admit she knew about the balika sangha.

Manika knew I was scared. "Would you like me to come with you, Shanti?"

I shook my head. "I have to do this myself."

"Here, take some more sweets we made yesterday," Manika said, giving me a package. "Food always helps. Offer them to your father before he starts yelling at you."

She twisted a thin silver bracelet off her wrist and reached for my hand. "This is my good luck bracelet. I'll lend it to you. Touching it will remind you to be strong and stand up for the rights of all girls."

"Thanks, Manika. I'll tell you tomorrow what happened." She and Sameera both hugged me.

I hurried home and went to the back door. It was quiet in our yard except for some clucking from our chickens settling for the night. I peeked in the doorway. My father sat on a mat, staring at the front entrance. My grandmother sat near him mending a shirt, and Mother lay on the bed, feeding the baby.

I stepped into the room. All three adults stared at me. I looked at each one for a second and then focused on my father.

Father cleared his throat. "Sit down, Shanti." He pointed to a mat on the other side of the room. I sat down, placing the package of sweets beside me. As I put my hands in my lap I felt Manika's bracelet and covered it with my hand.

"I watched the drama," my father said, glaring at me. "I did not know you would be in it. Are you a member of the balika sangha?"

I nodded slightly and looked at my hands.

"How long have you been going to these meetings? What foolish things are they telling you?"

"We learn about our rights. We have a right to education, as the girl in the drama said." I twisted the silver bracelet.

"Are they telling you to disobey me and refuse marriage?" His voice was louder. "Look at me, Shanti," he demanded. "Answer me!"

I looked at him. "We learned that it's against the law for girls to be married before eighteen years," I stated.

My father rubbed his forehead. "But the laws don't protect young girls. If you are sexually assaulted, you'll bring shame on our family. Then no man will agree to marry you."

He stood up and looked out the door. "Marriage is better protection than the law. A husband gives you a home and safety. That's why I arranged your marriage to a good man."

What could I say? Did I dare to speak of wanting an education?

"Father, you give me a good home and you keep me safe. When I went to school in town I was safe, and we learned karate to protect ourselves. If I get a good education and become a teacher, I will earn a good salary and help my family."

The baby whimpered and Mother murmured to her. My father glanced at them and back at me.

"Shanti, I wanted to be in school when I was your age. But my father died and that was the end of my education. As the only son, I was responsible for my mother and sisters. Since that time, I've worked every day of my life in the fields. Your grandmother and mother have had to work too." He lifted his shoulders and lowered them slowly. His head dropped forward.

I felt sad for Father. I knew he'd cared for his family from the age of fourteen, but I hadn't thought about what he'd given up.

"Your father works very hard for all of us," my grandmother said, shaking her finger at me. "You should not give him any trouble, Shanti. You should be an obedient daughter and do as he says."

My father returned to the mat. "No more talk tonight. I'm going to sleep now." He lay down and turned toward the wall.

My mother left the baby sleeping on the bed. "Come to the field, Shanti," she whispered. I got the small water pot and we left the house. Grandmother followed us, grumbling about girls being disrespectful. Mother and I were silent.

On the way back to our house, Mother held my

hand. I knew she cared for me, but she wouldn't speak up for me if it meant going against my father. I lay awake a long time, feeling that going to school was an impossible dream.

Chapter Eighteen

My first thought on waking was to wonder what my father would say to me. It was still quite dark, but I could see the shapes of my family sleeping.

I tiptoed to the front doorway and sat on the veranda, with my back against the cool mud wall. The first hints of sunrise gave the clouds a soft shade of pink.

A shuffling noise startled me, and I looked up to see Father standing in the doorway. I gasped and my stomach tensed. He put his finger to his lips and sat beside me.

"Have you been out here long?" he whispered. I shook my head.

"I saw your mat was empty, and I worried you'd run away." It wasn't light enough to see his face. I wasn't sure he was speaking seriously, so I didn't know whether to smile. I just shook my head again.

"I was so angry when my schooling ended," he

said. "I didn't want to work in the fields. But I had no choice." He stretched his legs out. "Two years later my mother said I had to find a husband for my sister. She was pretty, like you, and we wanted her protected." My father sighed. "The man was much older than her and was good to her, but two years later she died in childbirth." Father put his hands over his face.

I put my hand on his arm. "Oh, Father, I didn't know all that. How sad for you and Grandmother."

My father looked at me and nodded slowly. "I thought finding a good husband was the best thing for you. But seeing the drama last night showed me child marriage is wrong. You should get a good education."

I was so surprised to hear his words. Tears trickled down my cheeks. "Oh, Father, thank you! I will study hard, I promise."

My father wiped a tear off my cheek with his thumb and cupped my chin in his palm. "I know you will, Shanti. You are very smart."

We both looked up at my mother, who had just come outside. She knelt beside me and whispered, "Why are you crying?"

"I'm crying because I'm happy. Father just said I can return to school."

My mother smiled and put a hand on each of us. "Then I'm happy, too."

I felt so different that morning. My smile got wider with thoughts of going to school again. As I prepared tea and breakfast, I heard my father telling Grandmother he'd decided to send me back to school and stop the marriage plans. She grumbled something I didn't hear and glared at me as I served her tea.

After they'd gone to work in the fields, I tidied the room. I tucked my sister in the sling, picked up the water pot, and went to Manika's house. She was sweeping her veranda.

"Manika, my father said I can return to school! He'll end the marriage plans."

My friend grinned. "That's wonderful, Shanti! What happened last night when you went home?"

I told her what my father said and that he'd changed his mind after remembering he too had wanted an education.

"Do you think the drama helped?"

I nodded. "Seeing everything acted out showed our rights must be respected. And watching the drama with a crowd makes everyone talk about the problem."

"I'll miss you when you go back," Manika said.

"I'll see you when I come home on weekends. And you'll be busy with the sangha," I reminded her. I took Manika's bracelet off my wrist. "Thank you for giving me your bracelet to wear. It gave me courage."

I picked up my pot. "I want to tell Sameera my good news."

I caught up with Sameera on the way to the well. She was glad to hear everything was better for me. I asked if her father had seen the drama.

"He heard about it this morning, and he asked if I was a member of the sangha. I told him I was, and then he left for work."

As we waited for our turn at the well, we listened to the girls talking about the drama. One of them had played the part of the father of the girl who refused to get married, and she was enjoying everyone's comments on her good performance.

Trupti was there too, not joining in the chatter as she usually did. She came beside me and said quietly, "I saw your parents watching the drama. What did your father think of it?"

It seemed like she really was interested and not

asking to be mean. I wondered what her mother had said about it.

"He didn't say anything about the drama. He asked if I was a member of the sangha. I said I was and that we are learning about our rights." I paused, not sure what else I wanted to tell Trupti. "He told me why he was arranging the marriage for me. Then this morning he said I could return to school and he would cancel the marriage plans."

Trupti's eyes opened wide. "He did? You're going back to school?"

I nodded, grinning. "I'm so glad."

"Who'll look after your baby sister?"

She surprised me with that question. I hadn't thought about that, and there hadn't been time this morning to discuss any details about school.

"Maybe Manika could take care of her," Sameera said. "She has her brothers to look after, so she might be fine with one more little one."

"That's a good idea, Sameera. My parents haven't talked about what they'll do when I'm away at school."

I asked Trupti, "Did your mother see the whole Kalajatha?"

Trupti nodded slowly. "She did. I was afraid she'd yell like she did in our meeting. So I talked with her before it started and asked her not to embarrass me again." Trupti filled her pot. "I reminded her I am one of the sangha leaders and I have to show I'm responsible. She's proud I was chosen."

I was impressed with Trupti's actions. "I'm sure you'll be a good leader," I said.

I stopped at Manika's house on my way home. I asked her if she could look after my baby sister while I was at school. She agreed and I was glad to have a good suggestion for my parents.

When I took the baby to my mother to be fed, I told her about Manika. She was pleased with that idea as she knew Manika was good with children. I asked what my grandmother was saying about my return to school.

"Oh, she grumbled about the extra work she'd have when you're away and how girls don't want responsibility." Mother smiled. "Don't worry about her."

"Did Father say anything to you last night before I came home?"

My mother gently touched the baby's cheek. "After the drama, he spoke of his sister and we talked about making a different choice for you."

"Oh, Mother, I'm so happy things are working out." I stroked my sister's tiny hand. "See, little one,

I told you everything would be better for you. My friends and I are fighting for your rights." I looked up at my mother. "When will you have the baby's naming ceremony? Has Father talked with the priest about an auspicious day? Have you chosen a name for her?"

Mother shook her head. "Your father has been worrying only about marriage plans for you. Now he can think about the baby."

"I wish her naming could be before I return to school. My friends would help me with preparations."

Mother put my sister in my arms and stood up. "I will ask your father about it. You must be patient."

Chapter Nineteen

Later that day I was preparing supper when Danya came into the yard. I jumped up to greet her.

"Why aren't you in school?" I asked her

"My grandfather was in town. He told me if I wanted to come home for the weekend he could take me back to school," she said.

"Oh, Danya, I have so much to tell you. My father is allowing me to return to school!" I told her all about the Kalajatha and the marriage plans and what was happening with the other girls. She had lots of questions.

"Come back to school with me in two days," Danya said. "All the teachers asked about you. The principal kept your space open, hoping you'd return."

"My father might let me go with you so he won't have to miss a day's work to take me."

When my mother came home, we talked about how the family would manage without me. "Your father will miss your good cooking," my mother said. "He agreed that Manika could look after your sister in the mornings, and I'll come home in the afternoons to prepare meals."

"Is he worried about losing the pay for your work in the fields?"

Mother smiled. "Deepama told him your school expenses will be taken care of by UNICEF."

Grandmother came to the backyard to wash after her day in the fields. "Shanti, everyone is talking about that drama your group did." She squatted beside me. "Trupti's mother said they're going to call off the wedding."

My mouth fell open. I was truly surprised.

"And the next girl to have marriage plans changed will be Sameera," she declared, shaking a finger. "I saw Trupti's mother talking to Sameera's grandmother."

I still said nothing, wondering if my grandmother was angry with me for causing disruption in the village.

"I told the others working beside me that my son knows girls should have a good education," she said. "I told them you are very smart, Shanti, and you'll be first in your class." She gave me a big smile.

"I will do my best, Grandmother," I replied. It was

hard to believe she was now saying girls should go to school instead of getting married.

She went into the house. My mother covered her mouth to keep from laughing out loud. I grinned at her and whispered, "You were right!"

When I served my father his meal, he asked me how soon I'd be ready to return to school. I told him about Danya's grandfather and said perhaps I could go with him.

"I could ask him if he'll take you too," he said. "But I think you should go on the bus. Danya would go with you."

I was surprised but very pleased he suggested the bus. "Whatever you say, Father."

I wanted to talk about my sister's naming ceremony, but I knew it was best to wait until my mother had spoken with him.

That night as I lay on my mat in the dark, I thought about how my life was now full of wonderful possibilities. I felt sorry my father had to give up getting an education, and it made me even more determined to do well in school. After hearing his story I understood him better, and it felt as though a wall between us had fallen down. I knew he really cared about me.

My grandmother's gentle snoring beside me

made me think of how her attitude toward me had changed. Instead of criticizing me and blaming me for causing disturbances in the village, she seemed to be proud of me for standing up for the rights of girls. I wondered if she had ever wanted to learn to read and if she'd allow me to teach her.

I was so grateful my mother had quietly encouraged me, even though she was afraid of my father's anger. And I'm so fortunate to have friends who'd helped to make these changes happen. The balika sangha brought us together so we'd have the courage to speak out.

On my way to the well the next morning I stopped at Danya's house. She got her water pot and as we walked I told her what my grandmother said the night before. I said my father agreed I could return to school with her but wanted us to go on the bus.

"That's wonderful. I'm so glad you'll come back with me," she said. "Do you think Trupti or Sameera will come to school too?"

"We'll ask them," I replied. Both girls were at the well, talking with Manika and several others.

Trupti waved at us. "Did you hear my wedding's been called off?" She grinned and clapped her hands.

"I see you're happy about it," I said. "Is your mother upset?"

Trupti shook her head. "She made my father cancel the agreement yesterday. She says we'll wait for a better groom." Trupti laughed. "I'm sure what she learned from the drama will make her wait until I'm eighteen to find the right man."

Sameera came beside me. "My father said the same thing, no marriage plans until I'm eighteen." She said to Danya, "Maybe I'll be going to school with you next term."

Danya hugged her. "That would be wonderful! Shanti's coming back with me tomorrow."

Sameera raised her eyebrows as she looked at me. "Your father agreed to let you go so soon, Shanti?"

"Yes, I can hardly believe it," I said.

"What does your grandmother say?"

I laughed. "Last night she said girls should get an education, and she expects me to be first in my class."

Trupti looked at me. "She's not angry that you won't be home to look after the baby and do the cooking?"

"Manika will help with my sister, and my mother

will be home in the afternoons," I said. "What about you, Trupti? Will you come to school too?"

She shook her head. "I've been out of school too long, and I didn't like it anyway. I've been helping my uncle in his tailor shop, and I like sewing. It's much better than working in the fields."

"Did you make the kameez you're wearing?" I asked. Trupti nodded. "It's beautiful!" I said, and our friends agreed.

Manika said, "Trupti and I have lots of ideas for our balika sangha to work on."

"One thing we'll do is build latrines," Trupti said. "And the first one will be in my yard!"

We all laughed, though I felt sure Trupti was serious about that demand.

I was busy that afternoon, washing clothes, weeding the garden, and cleaning the house. I spent extra time making a special meal. When my father came home I greeted him with a smile. It felt so much better than avoiding him as I'd been doing.

When I served his dinner he said, "I asked the priest about good days for the baby's naming ceremony. The earliest day is in a few weeks."

"How will we get all the preparations done with Shanti at school?" my grandmother asked.

"I'll come home a few days before the ceremony,

and my friends will help me with the food and decorations," I said. I knew Manika would be happy to have a project for the balika sangha that the girls would enjoy.

Chapter Twenty

After supper I collected my clothes and things needed for school. My mother mended one of my uniforms, and my grandmother was soothing my baby sister as we talked about the naming ceremony.

"Shanti, I'll give you money to buy a dress for the baby," Grandmother said. "I have that red fabric but no one to make it into a dress." She pointed to a folded piece of silk on a shelf.

"Trupti is very good at sewing," I said. "She could make a beautiful dress."

My grandmother smiled. "I'll ask her tomorrow." She twisted a thin gold bracelet off her wrist. "Shanti, come here. I want to give you this."

She slid the bracelet around my fingers and pushed it onto my wrist. "Never forget your family is working hard at home so you can go to school. You must do well at your studies."

I hugged her. "Thank you, Grandmother. I will treasure your gift and always do my best."

"Maybe you will be a teacher in our village," she said. "You could teach the older girls so they don't have to go away to town for school."

"It's good the girls have a balika sangha to learn about things," my mother said. I saw my grandmother nodding slightly in agreement.

"Mother, you women could have a sangha. Deepama and Bharati would be glad to start one in the village."

"Why do we need a sangha?" Grandmother asked. "We talk together all the time."

"Balamani's mother-in-law is a member of a sangha in their village, and she said the women support each other and help everyone solve their problems," I said. "They've worked together planting vegetable gardens and building latrines."

"Did Balamani have a latrine in her yard?" my mother asked.

I shook my head. "Not yet, but she will soon. Women in their sangha who can read and write are teaching the others. I told Balamani she could help with that."

Manika and Sameera came to our door, bringing some sweets for me to take to school. We told them about the naming ceremony, and they said the girls in the sangha could perform the dance. My grandmother was very pleased to hear that.

I got up early the next morning, excited about returning to school. I washed my hair, braided it, and had my breakfast. My clothes were folded, with my two uniforms on the top. I laid the pile on my blanket and wrapped everything into a neat bundle.

"Come, Shanti," my father said, picking up my bundle. "I'll walk with you to the road where the bus stops."

I kissed and hugged my mother, grandmother, and baby sister. Mother brushed tears from her cheeks. "I'm going to miss you, but I know you'll be happy at school."

I nodded and turned away so she wouldn't see my tears. I felt pulled in two directions and tried to fill my mind with thoughts of school. When Father and I came to Danya's house, she ran out, ready to go, balancing her bundle of clothes on her head.

We walked near the well where several girls were gathered. Trupti hugged us both and said to me, "I'm glad you got the balika sangha started while you were home."

"I know you and Manika will do a lot to make our village better," I said. "Next time I'm home I'll be happy to use the latrine you build in your yard."

The girls giggled. Trupti said, "You can laugh, but it will be done, I promise!"

My father hurried us on. A few other people were waiting for the bus. When it arrived my father gave me money for the ticket and some extra rupees. "Use this for school supplies."

I hugged him and whispered, "Thank you, Father. I promise I'll do my best so you'll be proud of me."

He held my chin in his hand and said, "I am proud of you now."

I was the last to get on the bus. Danya pulled me onto a seat beside her as the bus moved forward. I stuck my head out the window and waved at my father.

"I'm glad we're going on the bus instead of my grandfather's ox cart," Danya said as the bus passed a cart loaded with straw. The one-hour ride felt like only a few minutes, as we talked the entire time.

We got off the bus a short way from the school. Danya and I walked to the office and greeted Mrs. Das, the schoolmistress.

"Shanti, I'm very happy to see you," she said, squeezing my shoulders. "You can put your things in the dormitory and join the others. Classes just started."

I couldn't help smiling all through my classes, feeling so grateful to be in school instead of working at home.

At lunchtime I sat on a mat with my plate of rice and lentils, thinking how nice it was to eat a meal I hadn't prepared. And even better, to eat beside friends to laugh and talk with, instead of worrying about being scolded by my grandmother for something.

Danya and I washed the dishes we used and returned to our dorm. In our room, a girl I didn't know was sitting cross-legged on the bunk below mine, looking very sad. I looked at Danya, raising my eyebrows, wondering if she knew her. Danya shrugged and shook her head.

I smiled at the girl. "I'm Shanti, and this is Danya. What's your name?"

"Nalini," she whispered.

"Did you just get here? We finished lunch, but if you're hungry, we can take you to the kitchen to get something to eat."

"I'm not hungry," Nalini said. "My uncle brought

me here from my village. Mrs. Das said to wait here until some girls came back from lunch to show me what to do. Are you in this room?"

"Yes," I answered. "I have the bunk above you. And Danya has the one beside me."

"There wasn't any bedding here," Nalini said, patting the mattress. "Is this where I should sleep?"

Danya nodded. "A girl left last week to get married, so that bed's free. Where does your family live?" she asked. "Did you go to school there?"

Nalini shook her head. "I had to walk to the next village with my brothers. They still go there. But I was the only girl in the sixth form, so my family wanted me to come here."

"Why weren't there other girls?"

Nalini sighed. "Some are married, and others have to stay home because their parents won't let them walk that far."

"It's the same in our village," I said. "But we're going to make things change. We started a balika sangha, and the girls are demanding their rights." I told her about our sangha and the Kalajatha.

During the next few weeks I heard other girls talking about the sanghas in their villages. I was eager to tell Manika and Trupti about some projects our sangha could do, like learning first aid and self-defence. We could also have sports teams and help children with school work.

It was wonderful being with my friends at school, and I wanted to learn all I could to help improve things in my village.

Chapter Twenty-One

I had to work hard at school to make up for what I'd missed, but I was so glad to be studying.

The day before my sister's naming ceremony, Danya and I took the bus as soon as classes were over. As we walked along the path to our village, we waved at neighbours working in the fields. Danya started chatting with one woman, but I pulled her on. "Let's go, I want to get home and see everyone."

When I came to my house, I hurried to the backyard. I hugged my mother and picked up my baby sister and held her close to me.

As I helped prepare our meal, we talked about school and our family and preparations for the ceremony.

"Balamani is coming tomorrow morning for the naming," my mother said.

"She'll be so happy to see the baby, and all of you,"

I said, remembering how sad she was when I visited her several weeks ago.

My grandmother came into the yard and I went to greet her. She hugged me tightly. "Shanti, you look well!"

"I'm very well, Grandmother. I want to hear all the news while I finish preparing supper." Her stories were the best way to learn about everyone in the village.

She sat beside me. "You know I'm one of the leaders in our women's sangha."

I looked at her, and then at my mother, surprised she hadn't told me. "I didn't know. That's wonderful, Grandmother. I'm sure you're a good leader."

She nodded, clearly pleased. "So many women came to our meetings that we had to start a second sangha. Your mother is helping the women who want to write and read better."

"I'm so proud of you both," I said.

My mother grinned. "Your father now says the sanghas are a good thing," she said. "He saw the women helping to build latrines, and he promised to build one in our yard."

We were laughing when my father came home. He smiled at us all. "Shanti, it's good to have you home."

"I'm very glad to be here, Father."

After we'd all eaten, we talked about the naming ceremony. Danya and I had made plans for decorations. My grandmother said Manika and Sameera had been practicing the dance they'd do. She showed me a tiny red dress with a gold border around the hem. "Trupti made this, as you suggested."

"It's really lovely."

I asked my father what name he'd chosen for the baby.

"The priest suggested several names, but I haven't decided," he replied. "I want to give her a name that will bring good things for her."

I fell asleep that night surrounded by people I loved who truly cared about me and my little sister and wanted a good future for both of us.

The next morning I saw some of my friends at the well. I told Trupti the dress she made for the baby was beautiful.

"Are many people invited to your sister's naming ceremony?" Trupti asked.

"My grandmother wasn't planning to invite very many to a girl's naming," I said. "But last night she told me we must prepare lots of sweets and other things to serve."

Danya laughed. "She's decided girls must be celebrated, and she wants her friends to know how progressive her thinking is."

When I'd filled my pot, Trupti said, "Shanti, you must come and see the latrine we built in our yard. My father and others dug the pit, and some of the girls in the sangha helped us build the walls." As I walked to her house she told me about other projects of the sangha.

I returned to my house and swept the floors and the yard. All morning I helped prepare food with my mother and grandmother. While we were eating our lunch, I saw my older sister coming up the path. "Balamani's here!"

Mother ran to greet her. When Balamani came inside, Grandmother put the baby in her arms.

"She's so beautiful," Balamani said, gazing at her.

That afternoon while we prepared for the ceremony, Balamani told me about Meena. "I've been teaching her and some other children to write," she said. "And I've been helping some women in the sangha with their reading and writing."

"I knew you could do that," I said.

Three women arrived carrying trays of food for

the party. My mother said the women in the sangha wanted to make special sweets for the celebration.

Danya and Sameera came bringing coloured paper to make decorations.

"Do you have a cradle?" Sameera asked.

I shook my head and got a large basket. "We'll use this. It will be beautiful covered with flowers."

After we'd decorated the basket and the room, I drew a muggulu, making symbols for prosperity and happiness. I put a lotus in the centre and surrounded it with a circle of leaves and flowers. The border had eight sides, to symbolize protection.

Shortly before the ceremony my grandmother called us to gather around her while she bathed my baby sister and dressed her.

Our yard was full of guests when the priest arrived to begin the ceremony. My father brought him into our house. He sat on a mat opposite my grandmother and the baby sleeping in the basket. He began chanting the prayers for the ceremony.

The priest nodded at my father when it was time to tell the baby her name. Father leaned close to her and whispered the name in her ear three times. She opened her eyes wide and looked at him. He smiled at her and announced to us all, "This baby is named Anandani."

My mother and I smiled at each other, pleased he'd chosen a name that means "joy." My father put a tray of rice grains in front of me. "You write her name, Shanti," he said. I made the symbols in the rice.

A woman whispered to another, "Why did he choose that name? Girls in our village don't have a joyful life."

Grandmother glared at her and said, "Now girls can have a good life. Look at Shanti, how happy she is getting an education. Our girls in the sangha are doing good things for our village."

A friend of my grandmother's, the oldest woman in our village, knelt beside Anandani to give her blessing. She gently touched my sister's cheeks as she said, "May you be blessed with wisdom, goodness, and a happy life." Anandani gurgled and waved her hands.

Grandmother said her blessing for a long and good life. She slid a small gold bracelet onto Anandani's wrist. Grandmother started singing and all the women joined in.

Manika, Trupti, and Sameera got up and began their dance in a space beside Anandani's basket. They beckoned Danya and me to join them, and we followed their moves. Several women sang and clapped in time, and soon everyone was clapping.

When the dance ended, my father stood up to speak. "I thank you all for coming to this ceremony for our beautiful baby girl."

Then my grandmother asked me to get my friends to serve the food to the guests. We carried in the trays, some filled with a variety of sweets and others with samosas and pakoras.

When most of the guests had left, several of my mother's friends helped clean up. My grandmother chatted with Deepama, who had come to the ceremony and joined in the celebration.

"You must be proud of Shanti," Deepama said. "She helped get the balika sangha started, and the girls have made important changes in our village."

"Yes, she is a fine girl," Grandmother said. "And now the women's sangha also has projects to make our village better."

"It's good to see the women and girls working together to improve the health of everyone," Deepama said as she gently stroked Anandani's head. "This baby is fortunate to be in your family."

My father entered the house while she was speaking. "Anandani is fortunate to have a sister who is showing that girls are strong and smart," he said, hugging me.

"And she's lucky to have a father who cares about us," I said.

Mother said, "Your father tells everyone about his daughters. Balamani is already teaching, and you will be someday. Anandani may be a teacher too."

That night I lay on my mat feeling very content and peaceful. The only thing that could make my life even better would be to have a high school in the village so I wouldn't have to be away from my family. Maybe the sanghas would take that on as a project. Then I could be one of the teachers in a few years. I also thought about Deepama and what she was doing to improve the health of people in our village. Maybe I'd be a doctor or a health care worker.

It felt so good to know that girls can have big dreams that really can come true when they stand up for their rights.

Glossary

balika sangha: translates as "girls' group." These groups were established in villages in Telangana, India, in 2002. About 8,000 adolescent girls are members of about 400 groups. The girls discuss issues such as child marriage and teen pregnancy and support each other in solving their problems. They learn about their rights, work together on community projects, and enjoy social activities.

dowry: an amount of money paid by the bride's family to the groom; in India, a law was passed in 1961 prohibiting the giving or taking of dowry

dung patties (also called dung cakes): cow or buffalo dung mixed with straw and formed into cakes. The dried cakes are used for fuel for cooking food.

Kalajatha: traditional folk drama

latrine: toilet, often a deep hole in the ground in a small shed behind a house

muggulu: a design drawn on the floor at the entrance of a home using rice flour, to welcome those who enter; also called rangoli

namaste: greeting, said with the hands pressed together and the head slightly bowed; one of the meanings is "I honour the place in you which is of love, truth, light, and peace"

pakora: a piece of vegetable or meat coated in batter and deep-fried

paratha: an unleavened bread made from wheat flour and fried in oil

salwar kameez: an outfit worn by girls and women; the salwar are loose pants and the kameez is a long shirt. The kameez are colourful and usually embroidered. A dupatta (long scarf) is draped over the shoulders. Girls' school uniforms are often salwar kameez, with the kameez a solid colour.

samosa: a small pastry filled with vegetables or meat and fried in oil

sari: clothing worn by women, a piece of cotton or silk material five to eight metres long, wrapped around the body so that one end forms a skirt and the other end is draped over one shoulder

scorpion: an arthropod with eight legs, claws, and a segmented tail curved over the back and ending in a venomous stinger

Shanti: girl's name, meaning "peace"

UNICEF: United Nations International Children's Emergency Fund (now United Nation's Children's Fund). UNICEF works in many countries to improve the health and education of children. UNICEF is involved in a global campaign to end child marriage; in India the fieldworkers help form balika sanghas and offer financial support to families so their daughters can continue their education.

water buffalo: a large bovine animal, used to pull carts; its milk is much richer than cow's milk, and its dung is used as fertilizer and for fuel when mixed with straw, made into patties, and dried (see "dung patties").

Author's Note

I was born in India and lived there for seventeen years while my parents were working in Andhra Pradesh. I now live in Canada and have always maintained an interest in Indian events and issues, and I read many articles about girls who refused child marriage. When I visited India a few years ago, I met girls who were determined to continue their education despite challenging family circumstances.

Organizations working to eliminate child marriage, such as Plan International and UNICEF, focus on increasing girls' access to education, as girls who finish high school are less likely to marry early. UNICEF works with governments, focusing on increasing girls' access to education and health care services; educating parents and communities on the dangers of child marriage; increasing economic support to families; and strengthening and enforcing laws that establish eighteen as the minimum age of marriage.

The United Nations Convention on the Rights of the Child (UNICEF, 1990) includes the right to the best health care possible (Article 24), the right to an education (Article 28), and the right to protection (Article 34).

For more information:
https://www.unicef.org
The Convention on the Rights of the Child
https://plancanada.ca
Because I Am a Girl
https://tharuni.org
Combating Child Marriages, Balika Sanghas
https://www.girlsnotbrides.org

Acknowledgements

I am grateful to friends and my family for their interest and support through the years of working on this book. My granddaughter, Trinity Clark, read drafts of the manuscript and made thoughtful and perceptive suggestions.

Members of my writers' group in Dartmouth, Jackie Halsey, Peggy Pilkey, Vivien Gorham, and Marlene Stanton, offered valuable advice and encouragement. My special thanks to Jackie and Vivien for reading an advance copy and writing reviews.

Dr. Mamatha Raghuveer Achanta, founder of Tharuni, an NGO working for the welfare of girls and women in India, was very helpful in providing information. She suggested I send her a questionnaire for girls living in villages with balika sanghas, and she translated the girls' responses. Dr. Mamatha graciously agreed to read an advance copy and write a review.

I am thankful for partner publishing with Anne O'Connell and her team at OC Publishing. I appreciated Anne's genuine interest in my book and her thoughtful guidance throughout the process. My thanks to Marianne Ward for her expert and thorough copy-editing, and to David Edelstein for his book designing skills.

About the Author

Marcia lived in India for most of her childhood. She attended Kodaikanal International School in South India, and spent vacations with her parents who worked in Andhra Pradesh. After graduating from Acadia University in Nova Scotia, Canada, she moved to London, Ontario, where she raised her family and worked as an early childhood educator.

A few years ago, Marcia returned to India, visiting people she knew and places she had lived. A highlight of that visit was staying with friends at Bridge of Hope, a non-governmental organization (NGO) that includes a residential program for children from rural communities, vocational training, and a medical centre. Marcia's experiences in India, and talking with girls who were determined to get an education despite challenges, provided inspiration for this book.

Marcia is the author of *A Privateer's Promise* (FriesenPress, 2022) and *Far From Home* (FriesenPress, 2021), a children's novel about her school experience in India.

www.ingramcontent.com/pod-product-compliance
Lightning Source LLC
Chambersburg PA
CBHW030945210726

48290CB00007B/2327